The Green Mill Murder

Books by Kerry Greenwood

The Green Mill Murder

A Phryne Fisher Mystery

Kerry Greenwood

Poisoned Pen Press

Poisoned Pen Press
6962 E. First Ave., Ste. 103
Scottsdale, AZ 85251
www.poisonedpenpress.com
info@poisonedpenpress.com

Printed in the United States of America

To Martin Suter

For a good man nowadays sure is hard to find
—Eddie Green

Acknowledgments

I am grateful for the assistance of the Victorian Ministry of the Arts in the writing of this book.

My thanks to Trina Cairns for diligent research and to the Jumbo Jazz Band for great music and inspiring information.

Special thanks to Eugene Ball; banjo player and composer extraordinaire John Withers; and Jenny Pausacker and Nance Peck for role-modelling and encouragement.

Chapter One

Make my bed and light the light
I'll be home late tonight
Black bird, bye bye.

'Bye Bye Blackbird,' Ray Henderson

It was eleven by the Green Mill's clock when the cornet player went into a muted reprise in 'Bye Bye Blackbird,' and one of the marathon dancers plunged heavily and finally to the floor at Phryne Fisher's feet. She stumbled over him. His partner dropped to her knees with a wail.

The cornet player stopped mid-note. The tall Amazon with the bass gave one final, mellow plunk. Tintagel Stone stood up. The three musicians came forward as Phryne turned the man over with her foot and recoiled, dragging her escort with her. The jazz players bent over the fallen man, and a high female voice, much affected by gin, screamed, 'The manager! Call the manager!'

'Come away, Charles,' said Phryne calmly. 'There is something seriously wrong with that man.'

'Why, you don't mean that he's…?' began Charles, and Phryne nodded.

It had been such a promising evening up until now, Phryne reflected, feeling Charles begin to tremble in her grasp. The monumental ceiling of the Green Mill glittered with electric stars. She herself glittered in a lobelia georgette dress with paillettes of Chinese white and diamantés. She had been dancing a foxtrot with Charles Freeman, sole scion of an extremely rich family, who was a tedious but socially acceptable escort. The two remaining contenders for the dance marathon prize (one baby Austin car, value £190) had been dragging themselves drearily around in ever-decreasing circles, requiring Phryne to dance carefully around them. She had been pleased with the dress, delighted with her dancing skill, and satisfied with her partner, who had been sufficiently snubbed to make him stop talking about his dead father's wealth and his own importance. She had been a little elevated on Grand Marnier, a flask of which reposed in her garter. She had been warmed by the admiring regard of the eponymous banjo player of Tintagel Stone and the Jazz Makers. His acetylene-blue eyes had been on her all night; they had produced an agreeable frisson.

Now she was stone-cold sober, and unenchanted, as she always was in the presence of death.

The dance marathon's surviving couple sank down, still wreathed in each other's arms, crying with exhaustion and relief and possibly triumph. Dancers milled about in the half-dark. Faces lit and vanished as the stars glittered. The manager glided onto the dance floor. He was a tall, distinguished man in perfect evening costume, worn with an Italianate air, and he summed up the situation instantly.

Dragging the marathon couple to their feet he proclaimed, 'The winners!'

They smiled sketchily as he hauled them bodily off the floor. After dancing for what seemed like years, they were so limp Phryne wondered that they did not sag out of Signor Antonio's grasp and melt down into aching puddles of ruined muscle. Both their faces were white and drained and they trembled as they stood on agonized feet. Blood seeped slowly out of the girl's shoes and stained the Green Mill's celebrated sprung floor.

'Percy McPhee and Violet King are the winners of the baby Austin car! They have danced for forty-seven hours and twenty-one minutes! Show your appreciation ladies and gentlemen, if you please!'

The patrons clapped appreciatively, Tintagel Stone's drummer gave a roll and a sting, and two waiters assisted Miss King and Mr. McPhee off the floor and into an alcove, where they were at last allowed to collapse. Miss King had begun to cry uncontrollably and Mr. McPhee did not seem far off it. They were set down on a sofa and fell instantly asleep.

'Signor, Signor Antonio, what about him?' asked a nervous waiter, pointing at the man on the floor. The signor flapped a dismissive hand. He had no patience with losers.

'Take him outside and revive him,' he said. The fallen man's partner, a girl in pale blue worn to a frazzle, ran her hand over his chest, made the discovery that Phryne knew she would make, and screamed.

'He's dead! There's blood! He's murdered!' She fainted.

And after that, of course, there was no more dancing.

The lights came up, revealing the Green Mill's dainty Dutch murals, all milkmaids and trees. Pallid faces, over-rouged or under-coloured, blinked in the glare. Nothing looks worse, thought Phryne, than a brightly lit hall which should be dim. And by God, most of the patrons looked as if they had crawled out from under the Green Mill, rather than entered through the door with a two-shilling ticket.

The girl in the pale blue dress was carried by the band to a couch, where a waitress attempted to revive her. Three bandsmen remained staring down at the corpse, the cornet player still holding his instrument out in front of him as if he had never seen it before. Phryne's escort was not proving to be of that sterling mettle which is expected of a Gentleman in a Crisis. Normally cold and aloof, he had cracked. Knuckles between teeth, he backed away from the dead man until he stumbled on the lower step of the bandstand, dislodged a cymbal, and sat down with a thump.

'I've never, I've never seen…' he whimpered. 'I've never seen a corpse before! I've never…'

'Well, well, pet, don't take on. Corpses can happen to anyone, you know,' soothed Phryne. 'You sit there quietly and have a little tot of this, and you'll feel better.'

She produced the flask of liqueur and unscrewed the top, pouring a liberal measure into it. This Charles took, trembling so much that Phryne had to hold both his hands and tip the spirit into his mouth. He choked, his eyes bulging like a fish, and Phryne patted him impatiently. Corpses, per se, did not discompose her. The evening looked like being more interesting than she had expected when she had accepted Charles Freeman's invitation to dance at the Green Mill, and she was not minded to be distracted by her escort developing the vapours.

'Bear up, man, it is not the dead you have to be afraid of. The living are much more dangerous.'

This produced another sob.

The blue eyes which had been observing her so closely all night were fixed on her now, and she turned from Charles to face Tintagel Stone's intense gaze. A pretty man, she thought, smoothing down her decorative dress, very pretty. Midnight-black hair and pale skin and lapis-lazuli eyes. She smiled and held out the flask.

'Have some?' she offered, and Tintagel accepted gratefully. He poured out a drink, gulped it down, and went back to the band-stand, putting his banjo carefully on its stand before holding out a hand to the bass player, who looked shocked. Phryne nodded, and Grand Marnier was served all round. The band retreated to their dais and looked around helplessly at the hysterical throng. The patrons, primed with gin brought into the Green Mill in defiance of all the licensing laws, were shrieking like an aviary full of bad-tempered tropical birds.

'What happened, Miss?' asked Tintagel Stone gravely, return-ing the depleted flask. 'Is that chap dead?'

'Oh yes,' said Phryne evenly, suppressing Charles' next whimper with a firm hand on his shoulder. 'And he has been murdered. Therefore we shall have to stay here until the police come, all very inconvenient.'

She heard a gasp behind her, and wondered which member of the band found this surprising.

'My name is Phryne Fisher,' she added, surveying Tintagel Stone with appreciation. 'Are you Mr. Stone? We may as well get comfortable. It is going to be a long night. Not, may I add, the sort of long night I envisaged, but a long night nevertheless.'

Charles gave another, more pathetic, choke, and shoved Phryne aside as he leapt up and ran. She was minded to be offended until she saw that his destination was the gentlemen's cloakroom, and was pleased that he still retained sufficient social grace not to be sick in company.

Tintagel Stone caught and steadied her. His forearms were very strong. A consequence of being a banjo player, perhaps? She rested both palms lightly against a beautifully muscled chest. Close to, his eyes were not lapis but sky-blue, and the wide mouth curved humorously. He smelt of wilting starched collar and orange liqueur, a combination new to Phryne.

'I can stand up by myself, you know,' she commented. 'And here come the cops. Oh, super!'

'Super? What's super about the cops?' snarled the cornet player, voice rising in mockery. 'What's good about the cops?'

'It's a nice cop,' said Phryne. 'It's Detective Inspector Robinson.'

Detective Inspector John 'Call me Jack, Miss Fisher, everyone does' Robinson entered the Green Mill with three attendant constables and was struck deaf by the noise. Voices ranging from lowest bass to shrillest soprano were clashing in a discordant symphony worse than Schoenberg. The huge hall was blindingly bright with every possible jazz colour. His entry caused a brief silence, then the din broke out again, voices exclaiming and crying and babbling on the edge of hysteria.

'If I handle this wrong,' thought Robinson, preserving his calm with an effort unperceived by his constables, 'there will be a riot, and the chief will have my guts for garters.' He walked into the middle of the hall and raised his hands.

'Quiet!' he bellowed in a great voice, and silence fell. He swallowed to regain his hearing and continued.

'Ladies and gentlemen, would you all sit down. There's no danger. I won't keep you long. But we'll all get home earlier if I have your full cooperation and some quiet. Thank you.'

There was a brief flurry as the dancers left the floor and conversation began again, more softly, and without the presage of panic. The crowd had drawn away from the figure lying quite still on the floor in front of the bandstand, as though fearing contamination.

'They needn't worry,' Detective Inspector Robinson remarked as he approached the corpse, regulation boots thudding like hammers on the sprung floor. 'Diphtheria's catching, but death ain't. Now, Sir, are you the manager? What's happened here?'

Signor Antonio, shocked out of his Italian accent, was wringing his hands and almost weeping with chagrin.

'In my establishment!' he whispered. 'It is too much!' His voice rose to a shout. 'You must find out who did it at once!'

'Oh, woe, alas,' quoted Phryne, perched on the bandstand. 'What, in our house?'

'Put on thy gown, look not so pale,' capped Tintagel Stone unexpectedly. 'I tell thee, Duncan's dead, and cannot come out of 's grave.'

Phryne looked her surprise, and he smiled a devastating smile, showing white teeth. Tintagel Stone, Phryne thought, would bear watching.

Detective Inspector Robinson sighted Phryne, sighed, and beckoned to her.

He was an unmemorable policeman, with mid-brown hair and mid-brown eyes, and he looked worried.

'Well, well, Miss Fisher, I ought to run you in for complicity; corpses bloom like daisies wherever you go, don't they? Did you see this?'

'Hello Jack, nice to see you, too. Yes, I saw it. Well, I was next to him, but I didn't see anyone stab him. Unless you think that it was really me, in which case you'd better put the cuffs on, guv'nor.'

Jack Robinson did not smile. He did not like mysteries. He was not wild about sudden deaths either.

'Police surgeon is on his way,' he commented.

'Why?'

'To pronounce life extinct.'

'I can pronounce to you now, Jack, that life is as extinct as it can possibly get. Poor man.'

The dead man was comely, youngish, with dark wavy hair on a round, childish head; a high-bridged Roman nose; full, rather sensual lips, and a bluish chin. Phryne had noticed him sagging into his partner's embrace, his face a mask of exhaustion and pain. Now he lay on his back with his feet to the band, his hands open and lax, his face calm and empty like the faces of all human husks in which the enlivening light has been doused. The only sign of injury was the round red spot on his left shirt-front where some long blade, expertly wielded, had pierced his heart.

Phryne bit her lip. He looked different from the first time she had seen him dead, but she could not bring to the surface of her mind what fact told her this.

'Dead as a doornail,' agreed Jack Robinson. 'But it's the procedure. What killed him?'

'A thin knife, I think, unless he just died of exhaustion. These dance marathons are a scandal. More like the good old days of the Colosseum than anything worthy of the twentieth century. I wonder that Signor Antonio hasn't brought in the lions.'

'He was in the marathon?'

'Yes, Jack, there were only two couples left. They had been dancing for two days, two days and nights. Criminal, isn't it? They were next to each other, blundering round in a circle, poor things, and then he fell. I tripped over him, the other two realized that they had won and slumped to the floor, and the manager came and proclaimed them the winners. I saw that this one was dead; he had that look, Jack, but before I could do anything sensible the partner discovered he was dead and screamed the place down. And there was something…'

'Something?'

'Something different about him, but I can't recall what. The band came down to see what was happening, and the girl collapsed and was borne off to a sofa. She's over there, in pale blue. Then we all stood about and waited for you to arrive.'

'Who could have stabbed him?'

'Anyone, really. They had the lights down for the foxtrot and we were all moving.'

'Ah, dear, this is going to be one of those cases,' said Detective Inspector Robinson resignedly. 'They always are when you are involved, Miss Fisher. I'll get my constable to take all the names and addresses of the patrons, and you rack your brains to remember who was near you, and we'll ask them to stay.'

'Only me and Charles, and the plump lady in puce with that stout gentleman, and the other marathon dancers. The band might have seen something.'

'All right, I'll speak to you later, Miss Fisher. Ladies and gentlemen!' he announced in his big, confident voice. A sigh of relief went up from the apprehensive crowd. At last, someone who could Take Charge and tell them what to do. 'I'm afraid that I'm going to have to cut short your evening's dancing. If you would all proceed in an orderly manner to the foyer. There's a policewoman to search the ladies. Then if you would leave your details with the constables, you can all go home. I would like a word, however, with anyone who saw this poor chap fall, or was near when he did.'

A swift sort and a scurry of footsteps, a flourish of robes and coats and furs—some chinking suggestively as though glass bottles might be concealed therein—and the throng in the Green Mill was reduced to a few witnesses, Phryne, some recumbent bodies, and Tintagel Stone and the Jazz Makers.

The foyer of the Green Mill was huge, as large as the great hall of the Exhibition Buildings. The patrons were recovering from their shock and beginning to speculate, gossip, go into hysterics, faint, laugh or feel quietly nauseous, according to temperament.

The constables wrote busily, and Signor Antonio stood at the door handing out apologies and tickets for next week's dance with distracted generosity. The main doors swung shut. The huge hollow space which was the inside of the mill made itself felt. Someone was stopping the sails, which turned when the hall was open, and their noise was also cut off.

Detective Constable North was suddenly and piercingly conscious of the squeak produced by his new boots every time he moved. He was an experienced and somewhat battle-scarred cop, recently transferred from Vice.

Phryne went back to sit with the band and for the first time remembered her escort.

'Where's Charles? He should have thrown up his heart and been back by now.'

'Is he your husband?' asked Mr. Stone, with every appearance of really wanting to know.

'He does not have that honour,' said Phryne absently. 'No one does. I promised his mother that I'd look after him and he is a passable dancer. Damn it, where can he be? Oh, Constable,' she called to Detective Constable North, whom she had met in one of her forays into Fitzroy brothels to search for lost girls. 'There's a gentleman in the...er...Gentlemen's who was a witness. He might still be sick, he has never seen a corpse before. Can you hale him out? He's been gone a long time.'

Detective Constable North flicked a glance at his superior, who waved a hand, and then padded off to the cloakroom, trying not to squeak.

'I think we had better be properly introduced,' said Tintagel Stone, impressed by her standing with the constabulary. 'I'm Tintagel Stone and these are the Jazz Makers. Ben Rodgers, cornet and trumpet.' A sullen young man with a fixed cigarette, dark eyes, and a lock of dark hair, Paderewski-like, over one eye. 'Jim Hyde, trombone.' A thin, wiry boy with pale hair and eyes who smiled like a slightly blue angel and must, Phryne thought, have lungs like bellows. 'Iris Jordan on bass.' A tall, slim, strong young woman who looked so formidably healthy that Phryne wondered what she was doing in jazz, a music redolent of late hours and smoky atmospheres. 'Clarence Davies on drums.' A muscular man with slicked-back brown hair, brown eyes, and a rather practised charming grin. 'Me, on banjo and guitar.' Tintagel bowed. 'And Hugh Anderson, saxophone and clarinet.' A wary smile from a terribly young man with longish brown curly hair who looked like he should not be out so late at night.

'Didn't you have a singer when I saw you last?' asked Phryne idly, wondering what Detective Inspector Robinson was making of the information he was receiving from the lady in puce and her husband. Instantly she knew that she had said something important. The band froze. The only one to move was Iris, who glanced at Ben the trumpeter, and then quickly away.

'Nerine,' said Stone at last, with a patently false air of unconcern. 'She isn't here tonight.'

'And why isn't she?' asked Ben angrily, flinging down his cigarette and stamping on it, then grinding the ashes into the Green Mill's expensive parquet. The question did not seem to have received an answer, so Phryne asked it again.

'Well, why isn't she?'

'Arr!' snarled Ben, and turned away. 'I'm gonna walk around. They can't ask a man to stay still this long!' He put down the cornet with loving care and flung off to circle the great ballroom, stalking like a caged creature. Phryne reflected that if Signor Antonio ever required lions for a Colosseum show, Ben would make a good acquisition.

'Don't pay any attention,' advised Iris, dragging a strong hand through her short blonde hair. 'He's not a bad old cuss but he's a trumpeter, and you know what they are like.'

The others nodded, as though at some received wisdom. Phryne didn't know what trumpeters were like, but she was willing to learn.

'What are they like?'

'They reckon that the brain gets starved of oxygen because they blow so hard.' Tintagel smiled. 'So they get bad-tempered and niggly. It's a showy instrument,' he added.

'But that would apply to trombone players even more, wouldn't it?' asked Phryne, looking at Jim Hyde. 'Aren't you niggly too?'

'No, Miss, but I think that's just nature.' Jim was certainly calm and gave the impression of being reliable, which is always an underrated commodity. 'Some of us have the temperament to be a trumpeter and some of us haven't, and that's a fact. How long do you think this cop is going to keep us?'

'He's just going to see the other marathon dancers. Poor things, they must be dead. Oops, I mean, they must be worn out.'

Detective Inspector Robinson was having some difficulty waking Percy and Violet, and, once they were awake, getting any useful answers.

'Did you see anyone near you when the chap collapsed?' he asked again.

Violet rubbed her face hard and tried to compel her escort's attention. He was sleeping quietly with his head pillowed on her shoulder and he appeared determined to stay that way. Jack Robinson was reminded of faces he had seen at some disaster: white, set, shocked by pain or grief into shapes which they would not resemble when thawed into life again. The girl was not pretty, but had nice eyes, now red with lack of sleep. The man was good-looking, with delicate bones in a face too thin from present exhaustion and past privation. He did not open his eyes when he murmured, 'There were the other two and a pretty lady in blue and a stout lady in dark red and that's all I can remember.'

Violet agreed. 'We were in front of the band. I saw the stout lady in cherry-red, and a dark-haired lady in blue, and then he just dropped; we realized that we'd won and we fell down in a heap too, and that's all we saw. Can we go home?' she asked piteously. 'We're all in. We can come and see you tomorrow. Please?'

It would be sheer cruelty to keep them, Jack Robinson thought. He took their addresses and sent them under escort to be taken home in a taxi.

The police surgeon had arrived, solemnly announced that the corpse was indeed dead, and been summoned to attend the corpse's partner, who still lay on the sofa, wailing at intervals.

'Well, Doctor?'

'Well, Robinson?' snapped the little doctor, who did not like policemen much, and who had been called away from a fascinating rubber of bridge just as he was about to squeeze his opponents out of three tricks which they should not have had anyway. 'The dead one is dead, and this one is almost dead. I've called an ambulance and I'll take her to hospital right away, unless you have anything to say about that?'

His moustache bristled, indicating that Robinson better not have anything to say about it. Jack knew the signs.

'If I might just ask one question…'

'No questions. I've given her morphine. She has a broken bone in that foot, for a start, or I'm no judge, and she's been dancing on it for two days. Later, Robinson, you can talk to her. Much later.'

Jack Robinson gave up, and went back into the hall in time to catch Detective Constable North returning to report.

'I've searched the Gents' and the rest of the place,' he announced quietly. 'That's why I've been so long. I found one side door open, and a few attendants, but I ain't found the missing gentleman. Miss Fisher's partner, Sir, appears to have done a bunk.'

Chapter Two

I went down to St. James Infirmary
And I saw my baby there…
So cold, so white, so bare

'St. James Infirmary' (folk song)

'Gone? Well, well, I never thought the man had the least particle of initiative.' Phryne stared at Detective Constable North in some surprise. 'Certainly never showed any before,' she added, a little disappointed. 'Charles gone? Are you sure?'

'Yes, Miss,' said the policeman. 'I've searched the whole place, kitchens and the usual offices and all. He ain't here.'

'Can you account for this, Miss Fisher?' Robinson had stiffened, like a hunting dog sighting lawful prey.

'No, except that he was terribly upset by the corpse. He ran off to the lavatory to be sick, I think.'

'Yes, he was very shaken,' agreed Iris. 'Staggered back from the dead one to sit down on the stand and kept whispering, "I've never seen a corpse before."'

'Thank you, Iris. Yes, he was so put about that he might just have run home to mother. And what she is going to say to me for allowing her little darling to be confronted with a corpse, I dread to think.'

'It ain't hardly your fault, Miss,' said Robinson. Phryne sighed and put back her hair.

'That will not make the slightest difference to Mrs. Freeman, who has never even been introduced to the concept of justice. Oh well, not to worry. Another problem for another hour, that is. Well, Jack, do you want to question us?'

'Yes, Miss, if you please, one at a time, and then you can all go home.'

'All right, who first?'

'Begin with the band, if you don't mind, Miss. You first. Mr. Stone, is it?'

Phryne resumed her seat on the bandstand, lit a gasper, and offered her cigarette case to the group. Miss Jordan refused indignantly, Hugh Anderson politely, and Ben Rodgers snatched one as he passed. The others accepted, and they smoked in silence. Phryne was casting about for something to say.

'How long have you been together, then?' she asked idly, wondering what Mr. Stone was telling Robinson, and where the idiot Charles had gone. Jim Hyde reached behind him for an illicit and hidden bottle of beer and slurped.

'Trombone players have a terrible thirst,' he explained. 'You could blow out your soul in a trombone. How long? Ooh, must be two, three years. I was playing with the Melbourne Symphony, very little scope for trombone. Then I heard some jazz, New Orleans jazz it was. We play Chicago, but what that man could do with that horn! And Tintagel was there, wanting to set up his own band, so I joined. We are actually making a living,' he added with faint astonishment. 'It's the new craze, jazz. People can't get enough of it.'

'I came over with Ten,' said the drummer, taking the bottle out of Jim Hyde's grasp. 'He comes from Cornwall, like me. We just got here and we met Iris, and then we got Jim, and Hugh wandered along—he's a medical student—and then we got Ben over spirited bidding from Tom Swift. I don't reckon he'll stay long, though, not since Nerine...'

'Look, what happened to Nerine?' asked Phryne impatiently. 'Did someone murder the girl?'

The band muttered. Hugh took the beer from Clarence and doused his blushes. Phryne waved a hand.

'Never mind, never mind, forget I asked. Doubtless all will become clear in time. Or at least clearer than it is at the moment. Off you go, Jim, the policeman is calling you.'

Jim obeyed the constabulary summons, and Ben Rodgers completed his ninth circuit and flung himself down, grabbing the bottle roughly out of Hugh's hands.

'What an interesting cornet,' said Phryne, noticing he automatically picked up the instrument. 'It seems to have extra bits.'

'Echo cornet,' said Rodgers in a deep, flat voice. 'It's got a mute built into the tubes.'

'So that's how you got that whispery sound in "Bye Bye Blackbird." I thought I didn't notice a mute.'

'No, well, I don't need one with this cornet. There's a valve on this side which cuts in the mute.'

'Can I look?' Phryne stretched out a hand, and he reluctantly allowed her to examine the cornet. It had a valve set low down on the left side, and a curl of brass tubing which ended below the bell, its outlet narrow and unflared.

'I bet it takes a lot of breath to blow that,' commented Phryne, trying not to mar the perfect surface of the highly polished instrument with her fingermarks. 'Fascinating.' She returned it to Rodgers, who breathed on it and polished it with his handkerchief, as though her foreign touch might have damaged it.

'You interested in jazz, Miss?' he demanded. 'You heard much?'

'Yes, I am interested. No, I haven't heard much jazz, unless you count a standing invitation to a New Orleans night in Gertrude Street, Fitzroy.'

'That'd be the Doctor,' commented Clarence Davies. 'Imagine you knowing someone like that, Miss!' He gave Phryne a smile which twisted wickedly at the corners. 'Imagine that, now.'

Fortunately Clarence was summoned before he could develop his theme. Phryne did not mention that her last case had required her to be more familiar with brothels than she would have liked. Instead she said, 'How long have you been playing?'

Rodgers replaced the cornet in its case with loving care. 'Ten years or so, what's it to you?'

'Nothing, nothing. This is called Civilized Conversation. I thought that you could do with a few lessons. We are trapped here until Detective Inspector Robinson has completed his inquiries. If you would prefer to prowl and snarl, my dear Mr. Rodgers, don't let me detain you.'

The band held their breath. Rodgers stared at Phryne as though she had dropped in from another planet. He drew a deep breath, as though about to bellow, then changed his mind and flung off to circle the dance floor again.

'You took a risk,' commented Hugh Anderson. 'He's got a foul temper, but trumpeters…'

'Are like that. What about you, Mr. Anderson?'

'I'm a medical student at Melbourne University, Miss Fisher, and I fell in love with jazz.'

'And he's very good,' added Iris. 'A natural with clarinet and sax. Only trouble is getting him to study enough to pass the exams. Then he'll be a real Doctor Jazz.'

Hugh blushed again. Iris smiled fondly on him.

'And you, Miss Jordan?'

'I'm a physical culture teacher,' said Iris, straightening her back and flexing a few muscles. 'Swedish massage and hydro-therapy and food reform, you know.'

'I'll never get a chance to practise on Iris,' said Hugh sadly, then recognized his double entendre and blushed afresh. 'I mean, she's so healthy. A bacterium wouldn't dare go near her.'

'Got my own practice,' added Iris Jordan. 'Old ladies and athletes, both obsessed with their bodies. A few months with me and they are healthy, all right.'

Phryne could believe it. Iris looked perfectly capable of forc-ing someone into health by sheer example. 'And I heard some jazz from one of my patients—Jim Hyde, who had trouble with his hands. So I gave him some exercises, and then I came along. The bass isn't so hard to play, though I still need music. The others just improvise. Why this cop wants to talk to all of us, I can't imagine. I didn't see a thing until Ten stopped us and went down to see what was wrong. I think he's calling me at last.' Iris crossed the floor to where Robinson waited with his constable and his note book.

Phryne was left with Hugh.

'Did you see anything?' she asked.

'Not really. I was watching the floor, like I always do, and I think I saw him fall, but that's all. I hope they won't get me in bad with the uni! I'm in fourth year now, start my internship next year.'

'Where?'

'Well, I was rather hoping to specialize in gynaecology. Pity the Queen Victoria Hospital won't take male doctors, though I can understand why. So it will have to be the Women's.'

'I know a doctor at the Queen Vic. Doctor MacMillan. She can give you a few pointers, perhaps.'

'Really? That would be wizard! We hardly see any real doctors, you know, only consultants who whistle past in a god-like state and then whistle off again. I think Iris has a point about medicine, you know. We tend to treat the disease, not the whole person. And she gets some amazing results. Science isn't everything, though don't tell any of my lecturers that I said so. Gotta go, Miss Fisher, the policeman beckons. Will we see you again?'

'Oh, I expect so,' agreed Phryne, alone on the dais.

Questioned and released, Phryne had paused only to press her card on Tintagel Stone before leaving the Green Mill and finding her car. The big red Hispano-Suiza, her extravagance and delight, was parked opposite Young and Jackson's, and her chauffeur Mr. Butler was asleep in the front seat, cap over eyes. The band, carrying an assortment of instruments and illicit bottles, were trailing along Flinders Street and passed her.

'Good night, Miss Fisher. Golly, what a motor!' exclaimed Jim Hyde, staggering under the weight of his trombone and four beer bottles. Tintagel Stone, bearing a banjo and a bottle of red wine, winked as he went on. They all smiled, except Ben Rodgers, who was carrying two cases and must have drunk his drink, because he alone was unencumbered with alcoholic beverages. Rodgers snarled, but Phryne was getting used to trumpeters.

'Had a good night, Miss?' asked Mr. Butler, waking up and pushing back his chauffeur's hat. Phryne climbed into the big car and tore off her beaded cap, running her fingers through her short black hair.

'Not precisely a good night, Mr. B, but undeniably interesting. There was a murder at the Green Mill, didn't you see everyone leaving early?'

'No, Miss, I been asleep, didn't notice a thing. What about the gentleman, Miss? Mr. Freeman?'

'Mr. Freeman has run away, it appears.'

'Oh.' Mr. Butler got out, swung the starting handle, and the racing engine turned over with a lion-like roar. He drove back to Miss Fisher's bijou residence in St. Kilda Road, casting the occasional sidelong look at his employer. She had been very upset by the last dead man, he remembered, but she seemed calm enough about this one. There was no accounting for women, he reflected, and swung the great car into its housing, cutting off the engine. Phryne leapt out, pulling her black evening cloak about her.

'I need a drink,' she said, and ran down the path to the back door, to be admitted by Mrs. Butler on a wave of warmth and the scent of freshly ground coffee.

'We've had another murder, Mrs. B, at the Green Mill of all places, and Mr. Freeman has done a bunk. So don't bother about supper if you please. Is Dot still up?'

'Yes, Miss,' agreed Mrs. Butler, who was proof against most domestic crises. 'She's in the drawing room, Miss, reading the new library books. A murder? Was there a fight, in a well-conducted place like the Green Mill?'

'No, no fight, someone was stabbed. One of the contestants in that foul dance marathon.'

'I've always said they was wicked things,' said Mr. Butler from the kitchen door. 'You go in, Miss, and I'll come and mix you one of my specials.'

Phryne went into the drawing room, warmed by the thought of one of Mr. Butler's cocktails. He declined absolutely to divulge the recipe, and mixed them in secret in the kitchen, but they were smooth, fruity, and authoritative. Phryne suspected kirsch and lemon juice and ice, but was unable to diagnose further.

'Miss! You're home early!'

Dot arose from the deep chair in which she had been reclining with three library books and a box of Hillier's chocolates, which she was eating at a rationed four an evening. Phryne threw herself onto the couch, flinging aside her beaded cap and cloak. She looked upon her maid and companion with affection. No one could say that Dot was modern. Her long brown hair was restrained in one plait down her back; her face was innocent of powder and her mouth of lipstick. She displayed a deplorably old-fashioned taste which ran to a chenille dressing-gown that looked like a bedspread, and sheepskin slippers. She was a disciplined soul, who would never eat a whole box of chocolates at one sitting and make herself sick. Phryne was very fond of Dot. She was infinitely to be relied upon.

'A murder, Dot, they always interrupt one's evening. And my escort has bolted, so wounding to a lady's feelings. That reminds me, I had better ring Mrs. Freeman before the cops get there. Back in a tick.'

Phryne kicked off her shoes and padded out on the cool tiles of the hall floor. She obtained the number of Mr. Freeman's imposing mama.

'This is Phryne Fisher, is Mrs. Freeman still up? No? Well, has Mr. Freeman returned? No again? Oh dear. Look, I really think that you had better call her. Yes, it is serious. Yes, I do know what I'm asking. Why? Well, there was a murder at the Green Mill tonight, and Charles left rather precipitately, and without an explanation or even a forwarding address. And the cops will be along any moment. No, I am not joking. Get on with it! She'll have conniptions if she's woken by the police. All right, I'll wait.'

Phryne sat down on the wrought-iron chair in the hall and began to wriggle her toes, reflecting that her new shoes had not done her feet any good. She could hear sounds of domestic upheaval over the phone; feet running, voices calling, doors opening and shutting. She ran over what she knew of the Freeman family. Two brothers, she thought, one killed in the Great War. Charles, the younger, cosseted when he became the only one. Rich family with pastoral interests who had made a fortune out of blankets in the said War to End War. Father popping off recently—heart failure, Phryne thought—leaving young Charles with two uncles still making blankets, and a large fortune. Pity he had few brains and very little style. She was wondering why no scientist had yet invented social skills in an injectable form when a sharp voice cut through her thoughts.

'Miss Fisher? What is this…preposterous story? Murder at the Green Mill? How could you have let my son…?'

'One moment, Mrs. Freeman. It wasn't my idea and I had nothing to do with it. There was a murder, Charles saw the body, and then went off his head, shaking and mumbling. He rushed off to the…rushed off to be sick, I think, and then he vanished. I rang to find out if he had come home.'

'He isn't here.' The voice was rocketing up into a screech. 'Charles! What can have happened to you!'

This, Phryne thought, was a bit tough on the poor unknown who had been murdered. Charles, as far as Phryne knew, was perfectly healthy.

'Calm down, Mrs. Freeman, nothing has happened to Charles but a bad case of the collywobbles.'

The shrill voice shrieked again, and there was a thud. A polite, butlerish voice took over.

'Miss Fisher? Mrs. Freeman has fainted.'

'So I heard. Well, call her doctor, and be ready for the cops. Mr. Charles seems to have disappeared.'

'Yes, Miss.'

'From the scene of a murder.'

'Yes, Miss?'

'So tell him to ring me if he calls and wants some help.'

'Yes, Miss. Will that be all, Miss? Good night, Miss Fisher.'

Phryne put down the phone and went back to the drawing room.

'Murder, Miss?' asked Dot, who had disentangled herself from her chair and was folding up the cloak. 'At the Green Mill? How do you feel?'

'I feel a bit shaken, but I'm all right, Dot, don't fuss. This is not the same as that other time. I didn't see this man die. I was just dancing past and then there he was, poor fellow, flat on his back and dead as a landed trout. He mustn't have known what hit him. What I can't understand is Charles Freeman's reaction. He went all wobbly, Dot, lost his marbles completely.'

'What was he shocked about, Miss? Did he see it happen?'

'Now that you mention it, Dot, I didn't ask him that. He staggered back from the body, sat down on the bandstand, nearly got crowned with a cymbal, and whimpered about never having seen a corpse before. I didn't have a chance to ask, either, because he shoved me aside and hared off to the Gents', and that was the last I saw of him.'

'Could he have done it, Miss?'

'Yes. He could have had the knife up his sleeve in a wrist sheath, like my throwing knife, and he wasn't holding me so close that I would have noticed the movement, not if it was very fast and skilled. I don't know, Dot, somehow I don't see that weak young man as a murderer. And I doubt very much whether he'd know exactly where to strike in order to kill instantly.'

'The man was stabbed, then?' asked Dot, privately wondering at how far she had come from the innocence of her mother's house. If, a year ago, someone had told Dot that she would be sitting in a lady's parlour in her dressing-gown, eating Hillier's chocolates and discussing murder without turning a hair, Dot would have laughed and told the speaker to get off the grog. She shut the chocolate box firmly and accepted a glass of lemonade from Mr. Butler, who was offering Miss Fisher one of his special cocktails in a sugar-frosted glass.

Phryne took the drink and sipped with fitting concentration. 'A work of art, Mr. B, as usual,' she commented. 'Sure you won't have one, Dot?'

Dot shuddered. She was willing to accept a glass of sherry, a whisky toddy when she had a cold, and an occasional cooling shandy, but could not fathom her mistress' interest in what Dot's tee-total mother would call Strong Drink. Phryne sipped again. Kirsch, yes, and a dark fruity taste; what was it? She gave it up. Every craft has its mysteries.

'Yes, stabbed in the heart with a sharp, thin blade. Very clever, Dot, because there was so little bleeding, and...'

'Were there Italians there, Miss?'

Phryne lost her train of thought. Something was nibbling at the edge of her mind and slid away again, like a flash of goldfish in a pond.

'Damn, it's gone. Something was different about him, Dot, and I can't remember what it was. Italians? Why?'

'They use thin knives, Miss. There's one in this novel I'm reading. Stilettos, they're called.'

Dot displayed the cover of *Murder in Milan*.

'You do have the most sanguinary tastes, Dot. No, no Italians. Signor Antonio is no more Italian than I am. Lost his accent directly he became upset. I suppose Charles might have done it, but I just can't see that he has hidden depths. However, the band might have seen something.'

'A jazz band, Miss?'

'Yes, Tintagel Stone and the Jazz Makers, and let me say that Tintagel is the prettiest man I've seen in weeks. The band are good, too; well, they have to be, to play the Green Mill. And the dance marathon is finished, Dot. Poor things, the winning couple danced for nearly forty-eight hours to win their baby Austin car, bless them. Though they will need Miss Iris Jordan's services if they are ever to walk again.'

'Miss Jordan? She's that physical culture lady,' said Dot, putting her empty lemonade glass back on the tray. 'You know, Miss, she has ads in the papers for massage and things. Mrs. Freeman's maid told me that they've done Mrs. Freeman a lot of good. Sitz baths, you know. She isn't well.'

'She enjoys bad health, Dot. The woman hasn't been well since 1915, and she's as strong as a horse. Well, well, that's a connection. Miss Jordan didn't mention that she knew Charles.'

'Perhaps she doesn't, Miss, if she only sees his mother.'

'Perhaps. Well, I'm going to have a bath and then I'm going to bed. Are you staying up, Dot?'

'No, Miss, I was waiting for you. What was different about the dead man, Miss?'

'If I could remember that,' said Phryne, trailing her maid up the stairs, 'I wouldn't have this uncomfortable feeling that there was something terribly important that I have missed.'

Chapter Three

The dead man smiled and brought a hand from behind his back. He held a bunch of flowers, which he offered to Phryne. They were red roses, buds and full blooms, and the scent was stunning. She moved closer, then saw with disgust that in the centre of one was a snail, a black and shiny snail which moved as she watched, slithering into the heart of the rose. Phryne recoiled, and the dead man thrust the flowers at her face. She screamed and woke up.

'Ooh, gosh, ghastly! My subconscious has a really unpleasant imagination!' She threw back the green sheets and leapt out of bed, dragging back the curtains so that the cool, pale light of early morning washed over her. 'Thank goodness for waking! The slimy creature in the heart of the rose, I wonder what it means? And I wonder what time it is?'

She found her watch.

'Six-thirty. I haven't been up this early for years. And I really don't want to go back to sleep, not if that snail is still lurking. I shall dress and go out for a nice walk. That'll astonish the neighbours. And Dot, too. It really looks like it means to stay spring for a while; October is an iffy month.' She found a dress and some sandals, washed her face and brushed her teeth, and caught up a handbag and house-keys.

Phryne tiptoed down the stairs and let herself out at her own front door with a click. The sun was rising, the sky was a fetching pastel barred with dark clouds, and the air smelt fresh. The esplanade was silent as she crossed over to the path that ran along the beach. One hardy fisherman hulked over his basket on the jetty. Phryne shook her head, losing the dark remnants of the dream.

The milkman's horse was clopping resignedly along the road when she returned from a brisk half-hour walk. There was a massive, tank-like clattering of bottles as the cart moved. The horse stopped at each house as though it knew the route better than its employer. Phryne stopped to pat it, marvelling at how huge the creature was; six feet high at the shoulder, and as docile as a lamb. It snuffled hopefully at her hands, its lips as soft as a baby's, and allowed her to stroke its neck.

'Morning, Miss!' hailed the milkman. 'You been out or going out?'

Phryne often met the milkman on her return. She felt unaccustomedly virtuous.

'Just out for a walk,' she called. 'Nice day!'

'Yair, it'll be a sunny one,' said the milkman, cocking an eye at the cool sunrise. 'Here's your milk, Miss. And one of cream. Gidday,' he said, hoisting a jangling crate of empties onto shoulders almost as broad as his horse's.

Phryne entered with the milk, surprising Mrs. Butler, who had just put the first kettle of the day on the stove.

'Morning, Mrs. B, I couldn't sleep so I've just been out for a walk. I ought to get up early more often. I haven't seen sunrise for ages.'

Phryne swept past the dumbfounded Mrs. Butler, and, collecting the newspaper from the front step, sat down in the drawing room to read it.

The papers had certainly enjoyed themselves with the murder at the Green Mill. There was a photograph of Detective Inspector Robinson looking as though he would love to run the photographer in for something, and of the Green Mill itself, with Flinders Street Station in the background. There was Signor Antonio, looking distraught. And there was a photograph of the dead man. Phryne read on:

> The victim has been identified as Mr. Bernard Stevens, a stock clerk employed by Myer. He was thirty-four years old and lived in lodgings in St. Kilda with some other young men. It appears that he was stabbed in the heart as the dance marathon neared its end. The winners of the baby Austin car were Mr. Percy McPhee of Carlton and Miss Violet King of South Yarra. They danced for forty-seven hours and twenty-one minutes before the marathon was brought to an untimely end by this dreadful occurrence. As yet, no arrests have been made, though Detective Inspector Robinson (pictured above) is said to be confident of solving the mystery.

Phryne smiled. Jack Robinson had not seemed all that confident when she had seen him last. However, things might have happened in the night.

There was just time to eat her breakfast and read the rest of the meagre information in the paper before the phone rang.

She had guessed who it would be before Mr. Butler called her.

'Mrs. Freeman, Miss Fisher.'

'Oh, Lord, Mr. B, I bet she wants me to go and find Charles,' she groaned, putting down an interesting column of spicy divorce news. 'Is that it?'

'Yes, Miss, I believe so. The lady is very upset,' he added.

Phryne went out to the telephone and said, 'Yes, Mrs. Freeman?' then held the receiver away from her ear.

When the shrieking had died away somewhat, she began to listen.

'Oh, he hasn't been home all night, and Charles is never away all night. What can have happened to him? And he was always delicate, if he's caught a cold it will go straight to his chest, and...'

'Listen!' yelled Phryne. 'Put a sock in it, woman, you'll give yourself hysterics. Now, tell me quietly. Has Charles not come home?'

'No,' said a cold voice, shocked into calm.

'And he has not called?'

'No.'

'And you don't know where he could be?'

'No.'

'And you want me to find him?'

'Yes.'

'All right. See how easy that was? I shall be over directly, Mrs. Freeman, if you promise to have a good stiff dose of valerian and a nice cup of tea and not to cry any more. All right?'

'Yes.'

'Who is your doctor? Have you called him?'

'Yes. He left me some drops.'

'Good. Take them, and I'll be with you in two shakes.' Phryne rang off and called to Dot to supply her with a hat and coat. The doorbell rang and Phryne, being nearest, opened the door.

Detective Inspector Robinson came in looking tired and lined. Phryne conducted him into the breakfast room and ordered strong coffee.

'Tea, if you don't mind, Miss Fisher. You going somewhere?'

'Mrs. Freeman has asked me to find Charles.'

'Has she? I can't find no trace of him.'

'Well, if I find him, I'll hand him over to you, Jack dear, though I cannot see him as murderer material. Do you want to talk to me, or can you wait until I've seen Mrs. Freeman?'

'I want to talk to you,' said the policeman with unusual abruptness. 'Mrs. Freeman can wait.'

'All right, Jack, of course. Mr. B, could you ring Mrs. Freeman and tell her I have been delayed? If she cuts up rough give her Miss Rousseau's address and tell her that she is a professional detective with more skill than I. Thanks. Jack, you look tired to death.'

Robinson shed his coat and dropped his hat and rubbed his face with hands which, he noticed, were dirty.

'Perhaps a bit of a wash and brush up, eh?' said Phryne. 'Guest bathroom is through there, yell if you want anything. Then you can have a brief and refreshing look at Mrs. Butler's new orchid—a cattleya, I believe—then a cuppa and you will be a new policeman.'

Jack Robinson did as he was told, washing his hands and face with Floris soap, and going out to the fernery to be shown Mrs. Butler's flowering orchid. It was a pink and white cattleya and it cheered his heart. When he came back to the breakfast room he absorbed two cups of tea without comment and sat back feeling, if not a new policeman, at least an improved one.

'Thanks. That really hit the spot. And that's a beautiful plant. Mrs. Butler certainly has a way with orchids.'

'She has a way with breakfast, too, if you're hungry.'

'No, I had mine at six. Boiled grease from the pie cart. This case, Miss Fisher, is, if you'll forgive me, bloody. I never had a case before with so many witnesses who didn't see anything! I've talked to every person near the dead man in that hall, and no one saw the murder. Even a good observer like yourself didn't see it. I can pinpoint when it happened—bar thirty-five in "Bye Bye Blackbird." All the band saw was the man falling. Three of them stepped down to pick the poor bloke up, and he was a goner. Does that bear out what you saw?'

'Yes. I had my back to him when he fell. He sort of fell straight back, stiff, dead before he hit the ground, I fear. I fell over him, his partner dropped to her knees, the other dance marathon couple fell down as well. In a moment the floor was covered in bodies. The band stopped playing and three of them came down, I remember; the trumpeter, Tintagel Stone, and someone else...'

'The clarinet player, Hugh Anderson.'

'Yes. And the man was dead then. I could see that he was dead. I said so to Charles and he backed away, sick as a dog.'

'And then he ran away and is still missing.'

'What about the search? Did you find the murder weapon?'

'No.' Detective Inspector Robinson chuckled. 'Lots of other things, though. Amazing how much booze people smuggle into a dancehall. A few penknives and so on, bottle openers, a couple of powders of unknown origin stated to be for headaches, usual stuff. But no knife. Nothing like anything long or sharp enough. We've searched the Green Mill top to toe and there is no sign of it.'

'I can think of one way that it could have been carried out,' observed Phryne. 'And I bet you missed it.'

'How?'

'Hatpin,' said Phryne shortly. Robinson inspected his fingernails and groped for his pipe.

'Oh, Lord, a hatpin. Could there be one long enough?'

'Dot? Can you bring down a bunch of the long hatpins?' yelled Phryne. Dot came down the stairs a moment later with what looked like a small armoury: cube-shaped, amethystine, jewelled, and enamelled. One of Phryne's hatpins, with suitable blade fixed, could certainly have stabbed Bernard Stevens, clerk, thirty-four, through the heart without pause or need for great strength.

'How could you hide it?'

'Put it back in the hat, of course. Did you search all the patrons to the skin?'

'No, well, they were searched for the murder weapon. I told my men to look for a knife. It is possible that...oh, Lord, it could have been missed. There were several ladies wearing large hats. Oh, well, if we missed it, we missed it. It wasn't on any of the people who were near, anyway; you were wearing that close-fitting thing, Miss Jordan had a bandeau, and so did Mrs. Winter, the lady in puce. The searchers would have noticed a gentleman wearing a hatpin. Though I didn't look at that frail girl in blue, the dead man's partner. She's still in hospital. Doctor says she's suffering from exhaustion and a broken foot. Name's Pansy Shore.'

'It can't possibly be,' Phryne laughed, then pulled herself together. 'What an unusual name. Well, sorry to give you another puzzle, Jack. Where have you searched for my errant escort?'

'His mother's house, his club, places like that. No one's seen him. So far there seems to be no connection between your Freeman and the murdered man. I don't know. What a case!' He had his pipe burning evenly at last, and sat quite still, staring without seeing at Phryne's marine-coloured parlour. Phryne said nothing. Jack Robinson reflected that she was a restful female when she wasn't raising hell, and shut his eyes for a moment.

He woke to the sound of music half an hour later. Strange but attractive sounds were coming from the phonograph.

'What's that?' he asked, hauling himself out of deep sleep.

'"Basin Street Blues." Well, Jack, if you don't want me any more, I'd better go and see Mrs. Freeman before she spontaneously combusts. Can I give you a lift anywhere?'

'Yes, you can drop me at my place.' He knocked out the dead pipe into an ashtray. 'I'm for my bed, at least for a few hours. Give Mrs. Butler my congratulations on her green fingers.' He stood up, grunting with the effort. 'And you will let me have Charles, Miss Fisher, if you find him?'

'He shall be delivered post-haste. Did you have a coat? Mr. Butler? I'm off to see Mrs. Freeman. Don't know when I'll be back. I'll call if I'm coming for dinner. Come along, Jack. And you can omit your usual lecture on speed limits,' she added, leading the way to the garage and packing the policeman into the big red car, 'I'm perfectly aware of 'em.'

'I never thought you weren't aware of them,' protested Detective Inspector Robinson as the car took the road. 'Just that you don't pay any attention to them!'

◇◇◇

Mrs. Freeman, a thin and agitated lady with advanced neurasthenia, was lying back on a chaise longue, smelling-salts and a small pile of fresh handkerchiefs to hand. Phryne was conducted into her presence by a resentful parlourmaid.

'She's taking on something awful,' whispered the maid. 'I never seen anything like it. See what you can do, Miss Fisher, she won't eat, nor take her sleeping draught, and Doctor can't do nothing with her.'

'Where's Mr. Freeman? Oh, I forgot. How long has he been…?'

'Six months, Miss, and she was getting over it. She never liked him much anyway, but Charlie is the core of her heart; real mother's boy he is. If she knew half of his goings-on she wouldn't dote on him so fierce.'

This sounded like it had personal application. Phryne glanced sideways and saw the maid's face screw up into a disgusted grimace.

'I could understand if it was girls,' she began, then dried up. Phryne searched for an acceptable euphemism.

'You mean that…er…he is unlikely to marry?'

'Yes,' hissed the maid. 'Boys!' Then she opened the parlour door, announced, 'Miss Fisher,' and allowed Phryne to pass in.

Phryne had always considered homosexuality to be unfortunate, robbing her as it did of the attentions of many artistic and beautiful young men. But she considered that it was as inevitable as being born with red hair, and did not approve of attempts to cure the sufferer, especially since the sufferer was not necessarily suffering and probably had no more desire to be cured of his propensity for pretty boys than Phryne had of hers. Poor Charles! That could explain a lot about him. Since he had a Dreadful Secret he would have to spend his life either frustrated or afraid.

Phryne wondered if Mrs. Freeman knew about this.

A moment's acquaintance was sufficient to convince her that Mrs. Freeman would not know anything she didn't want to know.

'Oh, Miss Fisher, excuse me for not getting up, but I'm so upset! Where can Charlie be? He never did anything like this before! How could he do this to me?'

This being a question with which Miss Fisher felt ill-equipped to deal, she ignored it and sat down on the edge of the chaise longue.

'What about his friends?' she asked. A gaunt, claw-like hand closed on her fingers, and she had to fight the urge to pull away. Mrs. Freeman's voice was ragged and breathy, as though she had damaged her throat with screaming.

'I've called all the friends I know. None of them have seen him. Bobby Sullivan—one of the County Cork Sullivans, you know—he laughed and said that Charles would come home if I left him alone, like Mary's sheep. He laughed! Charles goes around with rather a fast set of young men, Miss Fisher, frivolous young men, but not vicious.'

Sez you, thought Phryne vulgarly. I know these bright young things. They remind me that I'm not as young as I was. 'Yes, Mrs. Freeman,' she said encouragingly. 'Have you spoken to all of them?'

'Bobby is his special friend. He'd know where Charles is, if anyone does. Oh, Miss Fisher, I keep thinking of...car accidents, you know, and the river!'

'Is there a reason to fear that Charles might have...' Phryne paused, seeking an acceptable way of saying it, and opted for the most vague, 'done something foolish?'

It was not vague enough. Mrs. Freeman screamed and went into such hysterics that Phryne was forced to apply brandy and smelling-salts and another clean handkerchief.

'Now, listen,' she said roughly, 'if you are going to rocket off into the stratosphere as soon as I mention a nasty possibility, we're not going to get anywhere. Calm yourself. You won't last a day like this, and what use will you be to Charles if you're a rag? Come along, now. I shall order you some breakfast and you will eat it and then we will talk about Charles and you will not scream at me.'

This treatment seemed to be the right one. Mrs. Freeman stopped sobbing, Phryne gave the order, and the woman absorbed a boiled egg and three slices of toast and two cups of tea. The tray was taken away, and she was tidied by a voluble lady's maid who clearly disapproved of Phryne but was unable to say so, seeing that no one else had been able to get any nourishment down Mrs. Freeman's throat since Charles had vanished.

The maid left, closing the door with the suspicion of a slam, and Phryne asked again, 'Well?'

'No, he has never shown any signs of wanting to…do that.'

'What about drugs? Any suspicious white powders left in his evening clothes? Has he been elated or depressed? Think back. You should have noticed.'

'He was always the same to me.' Mrs. Freeman looked as though she might be about to start crying again, but glanced at Phryne and decided not to. 'He was sensitive, yes, always noticed if the eggs were overcooked at breakfast or the laundry hadn't starched his shirt correctly, that sort of thing. And he was out most nights with Bobby and the others, that's why I was pleased that you took him to the Green Mill, Miss Fisher. He doesn't know many girls, though that cat Mary Andrews tried to hook him for her pale, plain daughter. But of course Charles wasn't going to be caught like that, even though they have so much money. No, he's been just the same Charles. He was so good to me when his father passed on. He would stay in and read to me, and…he's my only one, since Victor…'

'That was his elder brother?'

'Yes, Victor. He was in the Gallipoli campaign. Such a sensitive boy, joined the army when he was just eighteen. There's a photo of him on the piano.'

Phryne walked over and looked at the young face, less pretty than Charles', with strong bones, a determined jaw under the small moustache, and deep eyes. He stared out at splendid battles under the ostrich-feathered hat, like a knight at vigil.

'And he never came back?' she asked delicately.

'Oh, no, Miss Fisher, he came back. But we lost him, you see. We lost him and we don't know what happened to him. Poor Vic! He came back very changed, couldn't bear the city, and went off wandering. We sent his cheque to a place in Gippsland for years, and he always collected it, though he never wrote. Then about four years ago the cheques came back. I don't know what happened to Victor. But there was Charles, you see. Now I've lost Charles, I suppose I ought to find out about Victor. But he was always an impatient boy, difficult and wilful, and Charles…'

And Charles, thought Phryne vindictively, was here to soothe mother and hand her the smelling-salts and tell her not to bother about an undutiful and probably shell-shocked son, who was moreover not as good-looking and possibly afflicted with unsightly scars of mind or body. So let poor Victor bear his load of horror out in the lonely bush, while pretty Charles takes his place in his mother's affections, and helps himself to the money and position.

'And you really don't know what happened to Victor?' asked Phryne, attempting and failing to keep incredulity out of her voice. Mrs. Freeman bridled and reached for the salts.

'He was safe enough, out there in the bush somewhere, and I could always reach him by letter. I used to write every year, on his birthday, telling him what had happened during the year, and how the business was going and how Charles…'

How wonderful Charles was, thought Phryne, how Victor wasn't needed or wanted, how he should stay where he was and not upset this nice domestic applecart. Oh Mrs. Freeman, you will be lucky if you don't run out of sons, if that's the way you treat them.

Aloud, she said, 'Well, Mrs. Freeman, what do you want me to do? I'm afraid that I've had to increase my fees lately. Cost of living, you know.'

'Fees? Miss Fisher, I understood…' Phryne gave her a polite but adamantine glance. 'Oh, yes, well, of course. Whatever you think fit, if you can find Charles. And Victor,' she added as an afterthought. 'I think that you might as well find Victor, too. If Charles is gone I might need Victor after all. He was last heard of at Talbotville, in Gippsland.'

'How long ago?'

'1924. Then the cheques came back.'

'And the letters?'

'Oh, I stopped writing,' said Mrs. Freeman casually. 'No point, if he wasn't there any more.'

'I see.' Phryne swallowed outrage. 'But what about inheritance? Would not Victor inherit, now his father is...er...passed on?'

'Oh my God!' Mrs. Freeman sat bolt upright. 'The will! Mr. Freeman never changed it! Miss Fisher, you shall find that Victor is dead! All of the business goes to Charles, but the house and the money to Victor!'

'You must have heard that from your lawyer. I suppose that there is a lawyer?'

'Oh, yes,' said Mrs. Freeman, 'But I told the lawyer that Victor was dead. For Charles' sake, you know.'

'For Charles' sake,' agreed Phryne. 'Of course.'

Chapter Four

Oh, Cholly, play that thing,
I mean that slide trombone.

'Trombone Cholly,' Brooks

Phryne treated herself to a large and indigestible lunch at the Ritz. She had been shaken by her encounter with Mrs. Freeman, and found that lobster stimulated her thought processes.

She looked again at the photograph of Victor Ernest Freeman, so lightly cast aside when he came home damaged from the Great War. A very pleasant face, she thought, reliable, honest, heartbreakingly young. Interrogation of Mrs. Freeman's acidulous maid had revealed that he had not been badly marked, just a white scar across the temple where a piece of shrapnel had failed to take off his head. But he had become abrupt, difficult, intolerant of noise and what the maid called 'the missus' silliness.'

'He was a good boy,' the maid had admitted, 'a better boy than Charles; honest, you knew what he was thinking. But the wicked war changed him; he wasn't the boy he had been.'

Of course he wasn't the boy he had been. Gallipoli had not been a pleasant or a successful campaign. Phryne decided that she would invite Bert and Cec to dinner and ask them about it.

But meanwhile, there was Charles. Where could he be? And what connection could he have to the dead man?

Phryne beguiled coffee and chocolates in contemplating her memories of Tintagel Stone, on whom she had her eye, then called home.

'Any messages, Mr. B?'

'Yes, Miss Fisher. Mr. Tintagel Stone called and asked you to visit a club with him this evening. He could not leave a telephone number so will call back.'

'Tell him yes. Anything else?'

'Someone called, Miss, and then rang off without speaking. It happened twice.'

'Hmm. I wonder if it was Charles? If it happens again, say that I will be at home and will answer the phone myself between six and seven. Can you call Mr. Bert and Mr. Cec and ask them to dinner tomorrow night? And ask Mr. Stone to dine with me at home tonight. Mrs. B might still have some of that delicious veal; if so, perhaps she could make breaded cutlets?'

'I believe that she has some left, Miss Fisher. The new butcher is coming up trumps. Would you object to dinner at seven? Mrs. Butler wants to see that new picture.'

'Of course. Tell Mr. Stone, and if he can't dine that early make me a reservation at the Windsor. Thanks, Mr. B. I'll be back by six.'

She put down the telephone and walked out. A wander past the fashionable windows of Collins Street was exactly what she needed.

Phryne concluded a charming afternoon with the purchase of a beaded gown patterned with peacock feathers from Mme Fleurette, at a sum which was really quite reasonable if you considered how many seamstresses must have been needed to sew on all those beads. She sauntered down Collins Street to collect her car so that she would be home in time to wait by the phone at the required time. It was about five when she arrived, time to have a cup of tea and try on the new dress.

'Oh, Miss!' exclaimed Dot. 'It's beautiful!'

'It's not bad, is it Dot? Love the way it dips down to the heels at the back.'

'Almost no back, Miss, you'd better wait until it's warmer to wear it. Who's the man, Miss?'

'Mm? Oh, that's Charles Freeman's missing brother. I'll tell you all about it when I have a faint idea of what I'm going to do to find him. What do you think, Dot?'

'It's not a pretty face,' said Dot, tilting the frame so that sunlight fell on the picture. 'But I'd trust him. A nice dependable face.' She put the photo on Phryne's bedside table. 'What's he done, Miss?'

'He's gone missing. And so has his bothersome brother. And how I am to locate one or both, Dot, I really don't know. However, I daresay something will occur to me. Did Mr. Stone call?'

'Yes, Miss, and he can dine tonight. I hope you find him.'

'Who? Mr. Stone?'

'No, Miss, the boy in the photo. I like him,' said Dot firmly, and went to run Phryne's bath.

At eleven minutes past six the phone rang. Phryne picked it up and heard someone breathing.

'Phryne Fisher here.'

'Oh, Phryne, what am I to do?' asked a frantic voice.

'You must come out of whatever wardrobe you are hiding in and I'll go with you to the cops,' said Phryne reasonably.

The voice gasped.

'Oh, no, I can't, they'll know by now.'

'Know what?'

'About Bernard. They'll know about him. Oh, Phryne!'

'Less of the "Oh, Phryne" and more information, Charles. What will they know? Where are you? And do you know that your mother is having whole litters of kittens?'

'Mother always does. She'll be all right,' said Charles dismissively. 'I'm safe. Don't worry about me.'

'I'm not,' said Phryne candidly. 'Where are you?'

'I'm hiding,' said Charles.

Phryne tutted. 'Yes, yes, I have already worked that out. What about Bernard, then?'

'He was…he was…oh, no I can't…' The line went dead. Phryne sat holding the phone for a moment, then hung up.

'Well, Miss, was that Mr. Freeman?' asked Dot. 'Do you want to wear the peacock dress?'

'No, I don't want to be too obvious in a club. Just the dark blue suit and a cloche, Dot. That was indeed Charles, who still appears to be panicking, but then, he's an expert. He says that the cops will know about him and Bernard, and in view of what that evil-minded maid of Mrs. Freeman's told me, I fear that Bernard was, er, very close to Charles. That gives the little ratbag a motive, of course. How commonplace. Never mind. Hand me that paper on jazz written by Percy Grainger and leave me to my fate.'

Phryne skimmed quickly through the scholarly treatise, noting that jazz was originally called 'jass,' and before that, 'jasm' or 'gism,' a word which Mr. Grainger declined to define but which clearly indicated the sexual origins of the music. The clerics and Catholic mothers of five who denounced it as Negroid music full of African savage drumming and dark urges were probably correct. Jazz, the learned Grainger informed Phryne, was a true folk idiom, an encounter between the European harmonic structure of brass-band music and African pentatonic chant. As such, Grainger said, it was unique and to be encouraged.

He appeared to be alone in his opinion. Phryne wound the gramophone and put on 'Dippermouth Blues' and listened hard. Yes, she could hear it. The pentatonic scale left out the third and the seventh note of the European scale, and the Africans, attempting to adapt their own music to this new scale, were unsure about which note to put in, and so blues got its unique sound. Phryne felt a sense of enlightenment. She had fought a pitched battle at school to avoid taking the piano lessons that were the province of good little girls, because she was determined to be a bad little girl; now she regretted it. She might have made some subversive use of that musical knowledge, as had the freed slaves who found brass-band instruments as loot on battle-fields, and adapted the uncompromising oom-pah-pah of the polka and the march to their own needs.

Tintagel Stone arrived on time and dressed in evening costume which was, although a little threadbare, quite correct. Mrs. Butler had produced vegetable soup and breaded cutlets, as promised.

'You look very snazzy,' Phryne commented, passing the salt.

Tintagel Stone grinned.

'These are my working clothes,' he said dismissively. 'Tell me, Miss Fisher, how is your investigation going?'

'Mine? I'm only employed to find Charles, and his brother whom Mrs. Freeman has just remembered she mislaid some time ago. And I haven't the faintest where either of them are. Have you seen the police since last night?'

'Oh, yes, they've been through all of our lodgings, even through Iris' establishment. She was furious! But they haven't found anything.'

'What were they looking for?'

'A knife,' said Tintagel Stone, looking Phryne in the eye. This was a trait which Phryne had learned to distrust. She instantly concluded that Tintagel had something to hide, but most people had something to hide, and it might have nothing to do with the murder at the Green Mill.

'And they didn't find it?'

'No.'

'Good. Have some cutlets. I've been reading a paper about jazz,' said Phryne, changing the subject. 'I can see how it started, but how did it go on? And why New Orleans?'

'Ah. Interesting place.' Tintagel paused for long enough to pay silent tribute to Mrs. Butler's skill with cutlets. 'There was ragtime, that is, ragged time, in the nineties. Then circus bands and such began to play in barns and in towns, and they centred on New Orleans because it was French and had a tradition of popular music, and because Storyville, in New Orleans, had Creoles and Negroes.'

'What's the difference?'

'Creoles've been free longer,' said Tintagel. His voice had a concise delivery, rather crisp, with only the ghostly remnants of a

Cornish burr. 'The Creoles belonged to the old French planters, and were free long before the Civil War. So the Creoles looked down on the American Negroes, and that created a social friction. Jazz came out of conflict—it's a fusion of different musics. That's why, when it goes wrong, it goes horribly wrong. This place called Storyville was, excuse me, a brothel quarter. Brothels always have good music, and cultured Creole music and vital African music got together and we had New Orleans jazz. Then during the Great War the politicians decided that Storyville was a threat to the health of their navy, and closed it down. A lot of the jazz men went to Chicago, where there were white men playing jazz. The old New Orleans style used three instruments as the core of the band—trombone, trumpet, and clarinet—but the white bands were using all sorts of things: piano, violin, banjo. So we had Chicago style.'

'Which is what your Jazz Makers play.'

'Only real difference is the offbeat and the solos. Jazz men always want a chance to show off.'

He smiled deprecatingly. Phryne suddenly found him enormously attractive.

'Where are we going tonight?' she asked as Mr. Butler removed the plates and supplied apple pie and cream.

'The Jazz Club. It's a bit...'

'Sordid?' suggested Phryne, and he laughed.

'Garish,' he agreed. 'And only coffee served. It's hard to really jazz up a jazz band on coffee.'

'You manage, in view of the amount of grog you were carrying out of the Green Mill.'

Tintagel flinched, a small flinch which might have gone unnoticed if Phryne had not been watching him so closely.

'You can't blow a horn for hours without beer,' he said defensively. 'It takes a lot of breath and they lose moisture all the time. Even Iris agrees that beer is all right for the horn and clarinet players.'

'And how about red wine for the banjo player?'

He grinned again. 'I don't like beer. In Paris, the clubs always sold a really rough *vin ordinaire. Trés ordinaire.*'

'Ah, yes, I remember. *Vin du table* made of real table.'

'I learned a lot of good tunes in Paris. Call it nostalgia. So, you have been looking up jazz, Miss Fisher?'

'Do call me Phryne. Yes. Fascinating, and not much written. Percy Grainger is of the opinion that it is a new musical idiom.'

'Never heard of him—what does he play?'

'Mr. Stone, I never know if you're joking or not.'

'If I call you Phryne, you must promise to call me Tintagel. Actually most people call me Ten.'

'How did you get such a name?'

'My parents were on holiday, and I was conceived on the cliff at Tintagel. It could have been worse. My brother was conceived at Blackpool. Luckily they decided to call him Alexander.'

'Alexander?'

'Sandy, after the Sands.'

Phryne chuckled.

'Well, shall we go?'

'No, the place doesn't hot up until eleven. We might play some of your records. Well, well! Race discs, I do declare.' He turned over a Bessie Smith recording reverently. Phryne sipped her coffee.

'Blues,' she explained. 'I have always liked blues. So I asked a friend in America to buy the Race records for me. They are not on general release—Columbia must have had a failure of nerve. Now that jazz has caught on so well, I expect that they will be released again.'

Mr. and Mrs. Butler passed, on their way to the pictures. Phryne waved.

'Have a nice time!' she called.

The 'Empty Bed Blues' wailed from the phonograph. Phryne and Tintagel sat in silence as the gospel singer's voice lingered on each note, extracting maximum pain.

'No more, no more,' said Phryne. 'Or I'll get the blues. I've got some New Orleans stuff—play that.'

Tintagel wound the gramophone and put on 'Basin Street Blues.'

'Dance?' suggested Tintagel Stone. Phryne moved into his arms.

Prolonged contact with a smoothly muscled body and the scent of soap, starch and male human always had a devastating effect on Phryne's never-very-good control of her baser emotions. She detached herself reluctantly, and kissed her partner delicately on the mouth. She found that, unlike brass players, whose embouchure produced a callus on the lip, banjo players were delightful to kiss.

'Come on,' she said, taking a deep breath. 'We are going to a jazz club, remember?'

'Oh, yes, the Jazz Club,' murmured Tintagel Stone without marked enthusiasm. 'Perhaps another night?'

'Tonight,' Phryne insisted, and took his hand.

'Interesting,' she said. 'Your little finger has the callus.'

'Interesting?' asked Tintagel. 'That's the way I play the banjo. Steel strings, you know.'

'Strong forearms,' said Phryne. 'Hmm. Look, I can't spend all night surveying your physical perfection.'

'Can't you?' asked Tintagel, sliding a hand down her back.

The Jazz Club was suitably dark, and smelt of coffee. Phryne had left the Hispano-Suiza in Gertrude Street, locked, and had asked the patrolling policeman to keep an eye on it. Tintagel appeared to be well known. Several figures, undistinguishable in the gloom, waved at him to join them. He ignored them and threaded his way through the tables to the front, where a girl in a red dress which appeared to have been moulded onto her body was singing, accompanied by a drum, a bass, and Ben Rodgers on cornet. The blue wailing melody wound its twelve-bar way over and under the brass, jarring and beautiful. It was the lament of a whore, cheating her customers, exploited by her pimp. 'It's all about a man, who kicks me and dogs me 'round,' sang the red-headed woman in a breathy, over-strained wail. 'It's all about a man who kicks me and dogs me 'round, and when I try to kill him...' The cornet soared, the voice dropped into a dark-brown operatic tenor, throbbing with anger and fear, 'That's when my love for him come down.' The audience were listening with open mouths. No one had heard these blues in Melbourne before.

'She's amazing! Who is she?' asked Phryne. Tintagel sighed.

'She's Nerine, Rodger's girl. God, she can sing like Bessie Smith. If only...'

'If only? Come on, Ten, do tell me.'

'You can ask her yourself,' he evaded. 'If she wants to tell you. But she's pretty touchy.'

'I bet she isn't as touchy as good old Ben. But trumpeters...'

'Are like that. You're learning.' Tintagel appeared pleased. 'They are also crucial, though don't let the others know I said that. The core of jazz is the trumpet. And Ben can play like the angel Gabriel himself.'

Phryne had always envisaged the angel playing a version of Handel's *The Trumpet Shall Sound*, but was willing to be convinced. What Ben Rodgers lacked to make him angelic was the temperament. However severe, the angel Gabriel would never have scowled like that.

'So trumpeters are in great demand.'

'Yes, especially reliable ones. And Ben is reliable. Not agreeable, but he always turns up when he says he will. That is unusual. And he is my old mate,' he added. 'At least he doesn't insist on singing as well.'

'Why?'

'He can't carry a note and he sounds like he's singing from the bottom of a deep well.' Tintagel laughed. A waiter came, and he ordered coffee.

'You wouldn't want to drink the tea they serve here,' he commented. 'Hey, Nerine! Come and meet a lady who has just become your fan.'

Nerine blinked, patted the trumpeter on the arm, and came down from the stage, carefully. Phryne realized that she was very short-sighted, and was steering by Tintagel's voice.

'Nerine, this is Phryne Fisher.' The singer took the offered wooden chair and picked up Tintagel's coffee.

'You like it?' she asked in a deep, honeyed Georgia voice. 'I'm glad.'

She then seemed to run out of conversation. Ben Rodgers, stranded on stage in the middle of the next song, glared at Phryne. She smiled her sweetest smile at him. It had no effect.

'Nerine, I'm looking for someone, and you might be able to help me. I'm a private detective,' she began. Nerine put down the coffee cup, rummaged in her bag, and took out a pair of spectacles. She donned them. They were very strong, magnifying her brown eyes to Betty Boop dimensions.

'You are?' She seemed to reach a decision. 'All right. I help you if'n you help me. I wanna find my no-good man and I wanna divorce him.'

'You're married?' Tintagel Stone was shocked. 'Sorry. But I thought that you and Ben…'

'You got the truth, Ten. I wanna marry Ben, but I got hooked when I was sixteen by a low-down hound who left me flat, and where he went I don't know.'

'I'll see what I can do,' said Phryne. 'You give me all the details and I'll find him if I can, so you can marry Ben—although, have you reflected that he is a trumpeter?—and you will help me find the person I am looking for.'

'Deal,' said the singer. 'Ten, honey, can you get me some lemonade? Then blow. Me and Miss…'

'Fisher.'

'Miss Fisher, we got things to talk about.'

Tintagel bore his dismissal well, producing the lemonade and then going off to join one of his invisible cronies somewhere in the smoke.

'Well, Miss Fisher, the name of that man was Billy Simonds, and we got hitched on the 21st of January 1920, in Melbourne.'

'What's your full name?' asked Phryne, writing busily.

'Nerine Sinclair. I was born Nerine Mary Rodriguez. My mama liked flowers. That no-good Billy was born here and went to Sydney, I believe. No one's seen him 'round here since December 1920. Can you find him?'

'I'll try. What did he do?'

'He was a sailor. I always was a sucker when it came to sailors. I love them li'l bitty white hats.' Nerine smiled reminiscently. 'But I wanna marry Ben, he's my man now.'

'Of course. I'll find him if I can, but it might take a while. Sailors also have a talent for vanishing.'

'You do your best for me, honey, I need to find that man. I ain't all that too sure of my man Ben. Now, who do you wanna find? Seem like us women always longin' for some man.'

'Charles Freeman,' said Phryne.

Nerine choked on her lemonade, coughed, recovered, wiped her eyes and glared at Phryne almost as effectively as Ben Rodgers had done.

'Why you wanna find him?' she snapped.

'Nerine, before I die of curiosity, what did Charles do to you? I wouldn't ask what seems to be an indelicate question, but I happen to know that debauchery is just not likely.'

Nerine took a deep breath, which had the effect of causing the nearest males to lose theirs, and shook her mass of red hair.

'You need to know?' The voice was ragged with outrage.

'I need to know,' agreed Phryne.

'He gave me the rush,' said Nerine in a voice redolent with fury. 'Sent me flowers, jewellery; took me out on the town, until I thought, I thought—this was before I decided to marry Ben. One night we were in his flat, the lights were down low and he was sitting beside me, and he said he had a proposition for me. And honey, I been expecting something like that, what with the diamonds and the orchids and all. But then, then…'

'Then?' asked Phryne breathlessly.

'He wanted me to sing in a new band! He wanted me to leave Ben flat and go and join this band which a friend of his had! I tol' him that I give Ten my word to stay with him. He laughed, one of them mean chuckles, and he said that women had no honour.'

'Oh,' said Phryne, uncertain of whether to laugh or not. 'So he never laid a hand on you?'

'Lady, I was expectin' him to lay a hand on me,' spat Nerine. 'Then I realized that he was one of them funny boys—we have 'em down south, too—and I flang his diamonds and his flowers right back at him and left the place. I swore I wouldn't never sing for him again, and that's why Ten has to do without me when he plays the high spots, because I don't never want to see Charles Freeman ever again in my life!'

'Where do you come from?'

'Georgia,' said Nerine. 'I came here with Billy—I told you that I was a sucker for sailors. Then I liked it here. Honey, if it wasn't for Charles Freeman I'd stay here forever.'

'He's vanished,' said Phryne, tasting the coffee, which seemed to have been made out of aged-in-the-wood beans that had worked hard for their living.

Nerine glowed. 'He gone? Then I don't have to go. I never been so insulted! To ask me to break my sworn given word! I'll have to tell Ben.'

'He knows. Flat, you say? Charles Freeman has a flat? Where is it?'

Nerine gave the address. It was, she said, carved on her memory.

'Nerine, did you tell Ben all about this, er, insult? Did he know about it?'

'Oh, yeah, well, he knew I was going about with Charles. He's awful jealous and we used to have some fine scenes. I tol' him I'd love who I chose. He didn't like that.' She chuckled, evidently a woman who throve on conflict.

'I bet he didn't. Weren't you running rather a risk, inflaming a trumpeter?'

'He wouldn't hurt me none, he needs my voice,' said Nerine complacently. 'I sing the blues better than any woman in this ole town. He knows that. But he was fierce against poor old Charles. I was right sorry for Charles, you know. Seemed like he didn't know nothing about girls. And he didn't,' she added with a vindictive snap of fine teeth. 'He didn't. Well, I've helped you as much as I can, Miss Fisher. Reckon you can find that no good man of mine?'

'I'll give it my best try,' promised Phryne. Nerine groped her way back to the stage and shook herself. There was a collective gasp. The red dress, which had ridden up, slid down like a glove over the voluptuous body. Nerine had an unrefined sexual presence that should keep Ben in a fine state of ferment for all of the time that she was in the public eye.

Tintagel came back bearing more lemonade.

'Well, did she tell you?'

'Yes, and I never heard of such a thing. However, I see your difficulty. I don't know whether I would have believed you, if you had told me. Now I have met Nerine, of course, it all makes sense. Let's go, Ten, I'm tired.'

'Home?' asked Tintagel hopefully. Phryne smiled at him, and this time produced the right effect. It was a smile of infinite sensual promise.

'Home,' she agreed.

Chapter Five

Dance, dance, dance little lady
Leave tomorrow behind!

This Year of Grace, Noel Coward

Phryne woke the next morning with her head on the banjo player's chest. He was sleeping deeply, naked and relaxed, still holding her so close that she had to exert all her strength to break his grip. He did have very strong arms. Phryne smiled reminiscently, got up, and pulled aside the curtains. Morning again, but it could hardly be called early.

Tintagel Stone was still asleep when Phryne was summoned to take a telephone call. She dragged on a dressing-gown, padding down the stairs in bare feet.

'Mr. Butler, if that is Mrs. Freeman again I will scream.'

'A Mr. Bobby Sullivan, Miss.'

Phryne took the phone. A light, pleasant, tenor voice asked, 'Miss Fisher?'

'Yes.'

'I hear that you have been retained to look for Charles.'

'You hear correctly.'

'Could we talk about it?'

'We are talking.'

'Perhaps, could I ask you to call on me?'

'Yes, that could be arranged. This afternoon?'

'Very well. At two.' He gave an address in the plush part of South Yarra. Phryne exchanged the usual greetings and rang off. Odd, she thought as she walked up the stairs again, savouring the soft carpet underfoot. Bobby Sullivan, of the County Cork Sullivans. She giggled. That was like saying the Birmingham Smiths: no distinction at all. Bobby had clearly exploited Mrs. Freeman's snobbery with a fine sense of irony.

Meanwhile, there was Tintagel Stone, and he would not have had time to get dressed yet.

Phryne got up again at noon, consumed a light lunch, and sent Dot down to the Public Records Office to search for evidence of the marriage of Nerine and Billy, and then to look for death notices.

'Why death notices, Miss?'

'I can't imagine any red-blooded sailor leaving Nerine for an extended time. The girl is the living image of "it." I suspect that dear Billy is no longer with us. If you can't find him we shall write to the other states. Bert and Cec are coming to dinner, so can you dine with me, Dot?'

'Yes, Miss, of course. Bye,' and Dot was gone. Tintagel pushed away his plate.

'I'd better go too,' he said reluctantly. 'We've got the Green Mill again tonight, lucky the management isn't superstitious. Shall I see you again, Phryne?'

'I shall be around,' said Phryne, kissing him lightly.

'I hope so. One person in a band singing the blues is quite enough.'

Phryne crooked an arm around Tintagel's neck and drew his face down to hers. The blue eyes blazed.

'I won't forget you, my dear,' she promised.

The mail was brought in and Phryne perused it over another cup of tea. A few bills went on one pile, some begging letters on another. There was a letter from Paris with news that Sasha was marrying an American pressed-beef heiress, which prompted a delighted chuckle; a letter from Bundaberg, Queensland, from one Peter Smith, most dear of anarchists; and a badly blotted appeal from someone who signed herself 'Violet King (Miss)'.

Phryne slipped the letter from the much-missed and loved Peter into her dressing-gown pocket, and read Miss King's letter carefully.

Dear Miss Fisher,
I make bold to write to you to ask you to tell the cops that we didn't have anything to do with the murder. The Green Mill won't pay up. I'd come and see you but I can't walk yet.

There was an address, and Phryne noted that there was a telephone number. She dialled it.

'Yair?' asked a shrill female voice.

'Can you take a message for Miss King?' asked Phryne politely.

'All right,' said the voice grudgingly. 'Who are you?'

'Phryne Fisher. Can I come and see Miss King at four this afternoon?'

'She ain't going nowhere,' said the voice. 'I'll tell her.'

Phryne then rang Miss Iris Jordan and arranged to meet her at Miss King's house at four.

'Now I really must get dressed, Bobby awaits. Funny how I detest the name. What to wear? Severe, I think. Dark green Dior suit and the emeralds.'

She dressed quickly, pulling on champagne-coloured silk stockings, camiknickers in black silk, a pale yellow blouse, and the suit, which fitted so closely that she never wore it when any action was likely. No one could run in a Dior suit. The shoes were glacé kid in emerald green. She examined herself in the mirror, pulled on her hat, a cloche with a drunken brim, drew in her eyebrows, brushed a little Rachel poudre riz over her nose, twitched her black hair into line across both cheeks, and smiled. Bright green eyes smiled back at her.

'Very nice,' she commented. 'You look like a *Vogue* cover.'

She drove at a reasonable pace (not more than ten miles a hour above the speed limit of twenty) to the address given by Bobby Sullivan and was directed by a discreet card in Gothic print to the top floor of an old Victorian house, turned recently and with taste into two apartments.

She rang the doorbell and was ushered by a pale, immaculate young man into a décor which mixed modern with antique in a pleasant, unsurprising, artistic mélange.

The walls were washed pale peach and hung with silk tapestries. The furniture included the usual Deco angular pieces side by side with carved Chinese blackwood, and a thick Persian carpet covered the floor.

'Do sit down, Miss Fisher. The sofa is very comfortable. Would you like some tea?'

'No, thank you, I've just had lunch. So, Mr. Sullivan, what can I do for you?'

'Charles,' said Bobby Sullivan, sinking, as far as was possible, into a Deco chair remarkable for its cubism. 'I wanted to talk to you about Charles.'

'Ah, yes. You are his great friend.' Phryne produced the phrase without irony or emphasis. 'Tell me about him.'

'He was not…my lover.' The young man cast Phryne a quick beseeching glance. 'My tastes…are the same as yours, Miss Fisher.'

'What was wrong with Charles, then?' asked Phryne. 'He's attractive enough.'

'Oh, yes, attractive, certainly. But he did not want me. Cold, Charles is cold, and cruel.'

Phryne leaned back in the sumptuous sofa and lit a cigarette.

'I never asked to be like I am,' he said quietly. 'I was born like this, with these emotions, with this heart. I was five when I first fell in love with another boy; one of the sons of my mother's best friend. He didn't love me, but that didn't matter. I wasn't interested in football at school, but in music and art. I was lucky that I found a congenial profession that makes me a good living. I design interiors for rich people's houses. I charge them a fortune, and so I can have my Persian carpets and my Earl Grey tea and my agreeable little suppers. I would marry if I could but I can't. I feel about making love to a woman as you do; impossible.'

'I understand,' said Phryne. 'You are managing beautifully, Mr. Sullivan. Dignity and restraint is the only way. With the occasional outbreak, of course. That is essential.'

'But I have to be so careful. I can't haunt the public toilets to pick up curious boys. I have a position. I'm living in a house of cards. One breath of scandal and they will all fall down.'

'I see. What did you want to tell me about Charles?'

'He is behaving in a very odd way. Poor Charles. He's… unloving. Not as clever as he thinks he is, either, and he plays games. He played one with me, making me love him, and then turning me down. He said some very cruel things to me.'

Phryne was suddenly very sorry for Bobby. Any lover might turn into a blackmailer, and the legal penalties for sodomy were biblical in their severity. What would happen to the exquisite Bobby in prison? Her mind shied off the terrible thought.

'Hmmm. I thought that he was homosexual, you know, because of his response to me. I do not wish to boast, Mr. Sullivan, but I am used to making an effect on a man, if I wish to. But all my powder was wasted on Charles, not that I really wanted him. I do not like games.'

'Charles does. He gloated over my broken heart. And I, too, am used to having my effect. We are similar, Miss Fisher, if you will forgive the comparison. And Charles has defeated both of us. By the way, that dark colour looks stunning on you. Green eyes are so rare that they should be emphasised.'

'Thank you. How long have you known Charles?'

'Oh, since school. He wasn't interested in sport either. He suffered a lot, I think, from the loss of his brother Victor. He was killed in the war, you know. Heroic figure, and Charles never felt he could live up to that. Then there was his mother. A vampire, I assure you: on the surface all fainting and smelling-salts and underneath pure prussic acid. She has hung onto Charles, using him like a husband, taking him into bed with her, clinging like a chorus-girl. God! The woman has no shame!

'But since I knew…' He paused, lit a Sobranie in a long holder, '…that I loved the same sex, I thought Charles was like me. He was never interested in girls, never had a crush on anyone, boy or girl. I should have known then that he didn't have the, the heart, I suppose, to love anyone. His mother has absorbed all of Charles' ability to love. I tried a couple of times to attract him, but he didn't even notice. Then when I asked him he laughed at me. But he stayed with me. He is very well read and very good company and very witty. He was always a bit of a hypochondriac, Charles was, prone to imagining that he had pneumonia when he had a cold, but that's not so unusual. We used to go to the opera together, Miss Fisher, and sometimes we would sit here and read aloud to each other like an old married couple. Absurd, isn't it?'

He brushed away a tear and turned his head to stare at the delicate dancing ladies on his Chinese screen. Phryne was touched.

She leaned forward and took Bobby's hand. It was a smooth hand, manicured, with a seamstress' much-pricked forefinger. Bobby dropped to his knees and buried his face against the pale blouse and cried in soft, heartbroken sobs, while Phryne embraced him gently, her chin resting on the well-groomed, dark head.

He cried for about ten minutes, then pulled away, groping in his pocket for a handkerchief. Phryne supplied hers, a large gentleman's monogrammed hankie which she always carried for the use of her clients. The young man dried his face and sat back on his heels.

'Sorry,' said Mr. Sullivan through the folds of the linen.

'Not all all,' said Phryne meaninglessly. 'I am very sorry, Bobby. I'll try and find Charles, but do you really want me to find him, if he has to stand trial for murder?'

'Charles?'

'Well, he ran away from the Green Mill, and the murder weapon is still missing. Did he have a reason to kill Bernard Stevens?'

'Oh, yes,' said Bobby, sitting down on the floor and leaning on Phryne's lap. 'Yes, he had a reason. Bernard Stevens was—well, I don't quite know how to describe him.'

'Try.'

'He wasn't…one of us, but he liked a little fling, with us. He had expensive tastes. He made a great play for Charles. He made Charles promise to be at the Green Mill to see the end of the dance marathon.'

'I wondered why he wanted to go on that day,' said Phryne, edging her thigh from under Bobby's sharp elbow.

'Yes. And there was another thing. He had pictures.'

'Pictures?'

'Yes, photographs. Taken at a party. There were some of Charles and Bernard, and one of me kissing Charles on the mouth—he would allow me to do that sometimes, if he felt that I had deserved it. And there are other photos of me. Really dangerous ones, which would ruin me utterly if they were found.'

'What do they show?' asked Phryne, very gently.

'There was a sailor, a boy from Glasgow. When Charles wouldn't let me do any more than kiss him, the boy offered, and I fell, and he was so pretty and smooth, and we went to bed together, and he…and I…and we were both naked and lying on top of the sheet and—do you know what they do to you for sodomy? I'll go to prison! And rather than go to prison, I'll have to die, and I don't want to die.' Bobby buried his head in Phryne's lap again. He wept briefly, sniffed, and looked up.

'So I have been sitting here for two days, taking panicky phone calls from Charles and waiting, waiting for the police to arrive. They must have searched his room. They must have found the photographs. They must know that…what I am. And I am just sitting and waiting.'

'For your house of cards to be blown down,' concluded Phryne. 'Not to despair. I know the policeman in charge of this inquiry. He is an old friend of mine. I shall get the photographs and return them to you if I possibly can. Where were you on the night of the murder?'

'Dining at the Windsor with a client. She had a million brocade patterns on which she demanded my opinion, and she took me home to her house and we went through every single one of the blasted things—all gaudy, vulgar rubbish, very expensive. I didn't get home until two in the morning but I did get the contract to do her country house.'

'Well, then, no need to worry. Detective Inspector Robinson is looking for a murderer, Bobby. He isn't concerned with other evidence of moral turpitude. Now, get up, like a good boy, mix a nice brandy and soda for yourself, and tell me why Charles can't be the murderer.'

Bobby, a little shocked, got up and mixed the drink as ordered, and drank it in one shuddering gulp. Then he smiled a weak and watery smile.

'Charles can't stand the sight of blood. There was blood, wasn't there?'

Phryne sat up straight. A piercing sense of something important that she had missed flicked past like an arrow and vanished.

'Yes, there was blood,' she agreed, dragging her mind like a fisherman trawling the seabed. Her net came up empty.

'Well, then. I can imagine Charles poisoning someone, if sufficiently threatened, I can imagine him hiring an assassin to kill someone, but I cannot imagine him sticking a knife into anyone. It's just not possible.'

'Hmm. And you don't know where Charles is?'

'No. He has been calling from public phones, you can hear the pips. I've called around all our mutual friends and no one has seen him. His awful mother called me, so I gather that she isn't hiding him. He has quite a lot of money, so he could be in a hotel somewhere. Please find him, Miss Fisher. He isn't the murderer.'

'I'll do what I can. About his brother, this Victor—did Charles say when he was killed?'

'On the Gallipoli campaign,' said Bobby. 'Yes. Charles said that his brother was an Anzac, and his mother was very proud of him.'

'I see. Did you board at school?'

'Yes. Why?'

'And Charles did not go home for the holidays?'

'Not home, he always joined his mother at some resort; she liked to take the waters at Hepburn Springs. Sometimes they went to the seaside.'

'Just Charles and his mother?'

'Yes. His father was always busy at work. Why?'

'Never mind. I must leave you, Mr. Sullivan. Don't worry yourself into a breakdown. I think that it will be all right. And I'll see you soon.'

Phryne paced down the stairs to the car, marvelling. What a mind Mrs. Freeman had! The unsatisfactory son accounted for, dead as a war hero, and used to taunt Charles. Holidays taken away from home while Victor was still living there. Careful explanations to Victor, presumably that his idealistic brother should not be exposed to a shell-shocked wreck of an adored figure. Cruel and vengeful and very, very clever. Planning of a high order. And Charles thought that Victor was a dead war hero, and that he was the only living son.

'Poor Charles is in for a shock, even if he isn't in for a hempen collar,' said Phryne aloud as she started the car. 'Assuming that Victor is still alive, which of course I don't know. I wish I could catch that memory!'

The big car slid to a halt in a winding cul-de-sac in the tattier part of South Yarra, and Phryne sat for a moment contemplating the house.

Someone had thought that an honest but simple Victorian terrace would be improved by blocking in both verandahs in order to cram as many tenants in as possible. The place was clean, smelling of sour yellow soap and flyspray, but it was cheerless and drear, painted a particularly depressing shade of dark stone. Phryne rang the bell, and a voice directed her up to Violet King's room. The stairs were painted, in lieu of carpet. Phryne began to understand how someone could dance their legs off for a chance to get out of this house.

Iris Jordan answered the door. In that shabby room, crowded with memorabilia of the tinselly kind, kewpie dolls and dance cards, she burned with a strong vitality. She had taken off her loose blouse and was clad in a skirt and a blue workman's singlet. Shadows slid over the perfect curved muscles in shoulder and chest.

'Miss Fisher? Glad you're here. All those stupid doctors have done is to give the poor mite morphia. Have a look at this.'

The frail girl, fair hair wet with sweat and face drained of all colour, was lying cramped up on a couch which would have been an asset to the Spanish Inquisition in making heretics talk. She was breathing fast through her open mouth; her eyes were dilated, black.

'What can we do?' asked Phryne. 'Shall I call another doctor?' Iris snorted.

'We have to get her unkinked, and now is a good time. You clear that table and drape this sheet over it, and I'll get that nightdress off. Poor little thing! If I'd got her at the time, before the muscles set, this wouldn't be half as bad.'

Phryne, as ordered, gathered an armload of magazines and assorted trivia from the table, placed the junk on the floor, and spread out the sheet, which evidently belonged to Iris. It was marked with her initials and was of a soothing pink. Iris was coaxing Miss King out of her nightdress and up onto her feet.

Miss King took two faltering steps on legs that were quite crippled and fell with a squeak of alarm. Iris caught her and lifted her, entirely without effort, onto the table.

'We've got to loosen those calf muscles, Miss King,' she said in her cool, matter-of-fact voice. 'Were you wearing high heels?' Miss King nodded, quite overborne by Iris' dominating presence.

'Silly. If you do such a thing again, wear flat shoes. Your calf muscles are knotted up like old leather.' Iris poured something oily out of a bottle into her cupped hand. It smelt powerfully of eucalyptus and pepper.

'My own compound,' said Iris, turning Miss King over onto her stomach. 'I only use it on athletes and horses. This will sting a bit,' she added. 'Just let yourself relax. You shall have your legs back in a few days, pet.'

Phryne watched as the strong hand smoothed oil onto skin that immediately reddened. Iris began to knead the thin legs, searching mercilessly for knots in the muscles. To Phryne's untutored eye the muscles appeared to be all knot. The girl's thin legs and bony buttocks upset Phryne, so she wandered away to leaf through the magazines and examine the pictures which covered all available wall space. Miss King, it appeared, was a movie fan. A large photograph of Douglas Fairbanks took pride of place. Next to it was a cabinet photo of a thin, intense young man; Phryne recognized Percy McPhee and wondered how he was faring. Clearly he did not live with Miss King. A piece of newspaper had been carefully clipped and glued to a larger sheet which was tucked behind the clock. It was an advertisement from the *Age*.

Phryne moved closer to read it, trying not to listen to the slap of hand on flesh and muffled moans from the patient.

> Small dairy and vegetable farm, Bacchus Marsh, own water, peach trees, house, ten milking cows, sheds. £200 or will exchange for a baby car.

Well, well, that was why Percy McPhee and Violet King had danced for forty-seven hours and twenty-one minutes, until they were almost dead and one of the other couple was dead. Could either Percy or Violet have been desperate enough to stab their rival? They were both very young, very poor, and might see this farm as their only chance at marriage and a happy future. They had certainly been at the end of their tether when Phryne had seen them; neither couple would have been able to keep on their feet much longer. It was a possibility. There were two problems with the theory. One was the murder weapon. Both of them had been searched and Miss King had not been wearing a hat. The other was the precision of the blow. Would anyone who had been dancing for nearly two days and nights have the strength to stab someone neatly in the heart and dispose of the weapon so effectively? Where had it gone? Phryne began to wonder if the murderer had swallowed it.

There was a knock at the door. A crone in a starched wrapper glared at Phryne.

'He's here,' she snapped, 'that Percy McPhee. And I tell you, whoever you are, that I won't have my house turned into a bad place by any fancy men. I won't have that girl in the house any longer, I tell you, not if he keeps calling. I tell you straight.'

'So you do,' said Phryne coldly. 'What are you talking about?'

'Her fee-anc-ay,' the landlady sneered. 'Out to all hours with him, didn't even come home for a whole two nights, for all her airs. Out she shall go, I won't have such goings-on in a respectable lodging house!'

'Oh, I do so agree,' said Phryne, forcing the woman out into the landing. 'Who are you?'

'Mrs. Garland. And I won't...'

Her voice drained away as she got a good look at Phryne. Money, thought Mrs. Garland; handmade shoes, emerald ear-rings, silk shirt, fancy suit. Mrs. Garland had never considered that Violet King might have friends like this. Phryne smiled slightly, allowing the impression to sink in.

'I've brought a masseuse for Miss King,' she said. 'She won a dance marathon, and I don't think she'll be cluttering up your respectable house any more. And I would like to speak to Mr. McPhee. That is out of the question in Miss King's room, as I am sure you'll agree. I'm sure that you have a parlour? Good. I'll just tell Miss Jordan where I'm going.'

Phryne called to Iris that she would be away for half an hour, and followed Mrs. Garland down the stairs to a cold Victorian parlour, perfectly preserved, from the slippery horsehair sofa to The Monarch of the Glen over the mantelpiece. A young man with a walking stick was waiting in the hall.

'Thank you, Mrs. Garland,' said Phryne. 'Come here, Mr. McPhee. You look all in. Have a seat. My name is Phryne Fisher, you may remember me.'

Percy, who was still drawn and walked with difficulty, grinned.

'I couldn't hardly miss you,' he said, easing back against the horsehair. 'I came to see Violet. Couldn't walk yesterday. Is she all right?'

'I brought a masseuse, she's with her now. Poor little thing was nearly crippled. She wrote to me. She was worried that the Green Mill might refuse the prize.'

'Yair. I dunno what we are going to do. You see, Miss, Violet and me, we want to go to the country. There's a farm at Bacchus Marsh we can swap for the car. It's our only chance. Violet's an usherette at the pictures, I'm out of work.'

'Can you manage a farm?'

'I'm from a dairy farm. I could milk before I could walk.' He grinned again. 'Come to the city looking for them streets paved with gold, but they was just plain asphalt. I reckon I can make a go of it. And if we don't make money at least we can eat. The dance marathon was our only chance. And we won it fair and square. Now them lousy…now they want to refuse us the prize. And I don't reckon we could do it again. Violet couldn't, anyway. I was carrying her for the last ten hours.'

'Yes, I saw you. You were behind me. And you couldn't have done it.' Phryne had a sudden picture of the position of the dancers. 'No, you couldn't have, you were behind me, Violet hanging on your shoulders. You were not in range of the victim.'

'Yair, well, I could have told you that. I told that cop. And I don't reckon I could have raised an arm to stab anyone. I wouldn't have, either. This is our future, Vi's and mine. Our whole lives, our chance. We couldn't start it with a murder. It would be all wrong. I want to be happy,' he said with quiet conviction. 'And I'm gonna be.'

'Can Violet stand the work on a farm? I bet she hasn't ever met a cow.'

'I think so. She wants to try, anyway. But if they won't give us the prize then it's all been wasted.'

Percy McPhee looked like he was about to cry, and Phryne felt that she had been cried over enough for one afternoon.

'I shall see the management,' she said, patting the young man on the arm. 'Don't worry. You shall have your car. And then Violet can give notice to Mrs. Garland. She will enjoy doing that, I'm sure. Have you concluded the deal with the seller?'

'Yair, I went out last week, bonzer little place. Bloke didn't want to sell but his missus has consumption and he wants to take her to Queensland. He's got relatives there. I don't reckon she's got long. So he's in a hurry to get out. Two weeks and we could be on our own farm. Married, of course,' he added quickly. 'We can get married as soon as Vi can walk again. She's had all her wedding things ready for three years. Got a licence and all. My dad says we can have the breakfast at his place in Rockbank, that's on the way. He keeps the general store—he got sick of cows too. But I reckon me and the cows are fated.' He grinned. 'You sure that you can swing it with the management?'

'Yes, I'm sure. Now, I'll just go up and see how Miss King is faring with the message. I'm so glad it wasn't you.' Phryne went out. A phone call should deal with the Green Mill. Phryne had a lot of social influence, to which all dancehalls were peculiarly sensitive. The powerful smell of liniment greeted her as it percolated down the stairs. Miss Jordan's compound, like Mr. Butler's cocktails, had authority.

Miss Violet King was standing up when Phryne came in; she had been clad in a new nightgown and was dubiously sipping a cooling herbal drink. Judging from her expression, it did not taste good, but she drank it anyway. For the first time since the dance marathon which was to secure her future, Violet looked as though she was emerging from a dark dream.

'Every hour,' instructed Iris, 'you will walk ten times around this room, and then you will lie down with your feet up. I'll be back tomorrow. I'm leaving some aspirin and a bottle of my mixture, all of which you will drink. You will feel better by tonight, but you mustn't go out and you mustn't get cold.'

'Yes, Miss Jordan,' murmured Violet. She glanced at Phryne, not recognizing her.

'My name is Phryne Fisher. I brought Miss Jordan, and I'll pay her, no need to worry about that. Percy is downstairs and is all right, though still limping a bit. Your prize is safe and the farm is arranged, so all you have to do is get better and be beautiful for the wedding.'

Violet stared at Phryne, still drugged, and strove for utterance.

'Now, I'm investigating the murder at the Green Mill, and I need to know if you saw anything, anything at all.'

'No, Miss, I was behind you. Of course, I recognize you now, the beautiful lady in blue. I was pretty far gone, Miss. I was just hanging on Perce. He was saying that it was the thirtieth time we had heard "Bye Bye Blackbird," and I was saying that it was the Duke's favourite foxtrot, just for something to say. I wasn't looking at the others, but I heard something.'

'What did you hear?'

Violet screwed up her lips and produced a sound. 'Pfft.'

'Pfft?' asked Phryne. Violet nodded. Iris turned from folding up her pink sheet.

'I heard that, too. Don't know what it was. Just before Ben launched into the mute reprise in "Blackbird."'

'Pfft, eh? I don't know. This case is going to drive me barmy. Anything else, Violet?'

'No. Then the chap fell, and you fell over him, and I just dropped. I never been so tired in all my life, never. Is, is it all right, Miss? About the car? And the farm?'

'Yes, and yes. By the way. Here's a wedding present.' Phryne took a roll of notes from her bag. 'Keep them secret. They are your little hoard.'

'For when things get bad, Miss?'

'No, with an experienced farmer like your Perce I don't think that things are likely to get appallingly bad. They're for you to travel to the nearest town,' said Phryne from the door, 'to go to the pictures.'

Violet unfolded the notes when the door closed. There were £20. She rolled them up and hid them in her underwear drawer, then limped out onto the landing.

'Percy?' she called, heedless of Mrs. Garland's sensibilities. 'Don't you come up, my dear, and I can't come down. But it's going to be all right, Perce. It's going to be bonzer.'

Chapter Six

Australia Will Be There
Australia Will Be There: For Auld Lang Syne.

W. W. (Skipper) Francis

'Well, Dot, you look pleased!'

'I found him, Miss!' Dot had discovered in herself a keen interest in diligent research of nice calm paper records, which never wept or ran away or turned nasty. 'I searched from December 1920 to July 1921, and then I found him.'

Dot displayed the death certificate of William Simmonds, which gave the cause as 'alcoholic dementia ten days heart failure one day' on the 11th of July 1920. Nerine had been free of her husband for seven years without knowing it. William had died in the charity ward of the Melbourne Hospital. He was listed as indigent, and 'not known' had been entered against next of kin.

'Oh, well done, Dot! Is that a certified copy? Super! That solves one problem. Have there been any calls?'

'Just that person who breathes, Miss. I told him you'd be back before six.'

'This game of hide-and-seek is no longer at all diverting. You are invaluable, Dot, really you are. Now I must just make a call to the Green Mill, and then we shall get all dressed up for dinner. Since you are dining with me, would you like to wear the peacock dress, perhaps?'

'Oh, no, Miss, I couldn't. But p'raps I could borrow the one called sunrise. I love the colours.'

'Borrow it? You shall have it. That gold and brown never suited me above half, but it will be just the ticket with your hair and eyes. You should have mentioned it before. And you can have first bath. Imagine, those villains at the Green Mill want to deny the prize to those poor dancers!'

Phryne stalked to the phone and obtained, after a certain delay, Signor Antonio himself. A brief pause while he identified Phryne, and then reassurances flooded from the phone. Of course Miss Fisher had no need to be concerned. Naturally the car would be awarded as promised. Certainly the young persons had won. The delay had merely been the whisper of a question about the incident which had ended the competition. Signor Antonio appreciated Miss Fisher's esteemed patronage. Could Signor Antonio hope for the pleasure of Miss Fisher's continued attendance?

Phryne assured the signor that she would definitely be back at the Green Mill, which really was the best place to dance in Melbourne, and rang off. Good. That assured the future of Percy and his Violet. Phryne wondered again what the sound could have been. Both Iris and Violet had heard it, so it could not have been an hallucination brought on by exhaustion. Pfft?

She gave it up and sat by the phone to wait for Charles, had a sudden idea, and called Detective Inspector Robinson.

'Ah, Jack, Phryne Fisher. How are you?'

'Terrible. This is a chronic case. I found all sorts of reasons why your escort should have killed Stevens, but I can't find him.'

'As to those reasons, Jack dear, I suppose that you are referring to photographs of the deceased and Charles in compromising positions?'

'I am. Nothing too obscene, Miss, but compromising. He had a wad of them stuck away under a floorboard.'

'Well, I'm not asking you to give me anything that is evidential, Jack, but if there are some which don't show Charles but do show another young man in a very compromising position, I suppose that you don't really need them?'

'No, I don't really need them. Why? You taking up blackmail too?'

'Was Bernard?'

'Oh yes. Polite, nicely worded blackmail, but blackmail all right. Nasty little piece of work. Got a couple of hundred pounds out of your Charles, I'd say.'

'Jack, he really isn't my Charles. I'm just trying to find him. And you shall have him as soon as I do.'

'All right, Miss Fisher, I'll have a constable drop round the other pictures, and the plates. I can trust you to deal with them properly. Otherwise I would have to hand them over to Vice. We don't want to prosecute them, poor nancy-boys, but the law says we have to. But find Charles for me!' Detective Inspector Robinson sounded ragged with strain. 'My chief is creating something fierce.'

'I'll find him. Thanks, Jack. You're a darling.'

Jack Robinson, in the course of his career maintaining Peace and Order for His Sovereign Majesty King George, had been called many things, but darling wasn't one of them. He blinked.

'My pleasure, Miss Fisher, and get a move on with that Freeman. I'll have to put out an all-stations hue-and-cry for him tomorrow if he ain't given himself up.'

'I'll do my best. Goodbye, Jack.'

Phryne sat by the phone, worrying. It rang.

Someone was breathing.

'Charles, dear, unless you give yourself up tonight I'm afraid that every cop in Australia will be looking for you. And another thing, tell me about your brother Victor.'

'Vic's dead,' said Charles, surprised into speech. 'He died in the Great War.'

'No, pet, your mother told you a little fib. Until at least 1920 your brother Victor was alive, and she wants me to find him.'

'You've gone mad!'

'Me, no, but I have my doubts about your mother. Now if you weren't snugged away like a rat in the wainscoting we would be able to talk about this and many other strange and wonderful things, but as it is, unless you put on your evening togs and come to my house at eleven tonight, I will advise your mother that I can't find you and throw in the case. I can't conduct an investigation sitting by the telephone. Besides, I hate telephones. I have seen your friend Bobby, who is a darling, and I know that the police have the photos of you and he kissing. They know all about it, Charlie, there is no use in hiding. If you didn't do it, my dear boy, then for heaven's sake allow me to prove it. If you are guilty, then try the port now, and get on a ship headed for America. Even New Zealand would do. Make up your mind. I haven't got all night; I've got guests for dinner, and I have to dress.'

'Vic's alive?'

'Possibly. Will you come?'

'I'll think about it,' and the phone went dead. Phryne slammed it down in a flare of irritation and went to see how Dot was looking in the sunrise dress.

She was so stunning that Phryne forgot her annoyance. Dot was fair-skinned, with fine brown hair and brown eyes. She doted upon autumn colours, warm browns, gold, umber, orange—a complete contrast to Phryne's preference for icy blue, dark green, purple, silver, and black. Phryne had bought the sunrise dress from a rather exclusive dressmaker because of its beautiful beading. The hem was the red and brown earth; the orb of the rising sun was gold, bright enough to hurt the eyes; and the sky was layered in red and orange, with a faint streak of cerulean blue at the shoulders. Dot had braided her long hair and twisted the plaits into a knot at the back of her neck. She wore brown stockings and brown leather shoes with a louis heel. Phryne surprised her staring at her reflection in the mirror, astonished.

'Oh, Dot, you look spiffing! That dress might have been made for you! Hugh must see you like this. Pity that policemen don't earn the kind of salary to take you to a place to match.'

'There's the Policemen and Firemen's Ball,' said Dot. 'I can wear it there. Anyway, I don't care if I never wear it anywhere. It might get damaged, someone might spill something on it.' She stroked the dress caressingly. Phryne went into the bathroom, shedding clothes as she went.

'Oh, Miss, I forgot. The girls rang. Can they go to the school Christmas treat? Apparently it's an extra.'

'Of course.' Phryne's adopted daughters, acquired in strange circumstances, were at the Presbyterian Ladies College, learning how to move freely among the Upper Classes. Having been poor, they were wincingly careful of Phryne's money, though Phryne wasn't. She found this trait touching and exceptionally unusual.

'Do they need clothes?' she asked through the open bathroom door, groping for the Nuit d'Amour soap. Dot turned on her heel, watching the immaculate colouring of the dress flow with the movement.

'No, Miss, but they want you to come to the prize-giving. In the Hispano-Suiza, Jane said.'

'The Hispano-Suiza they shall have.' Phryne remembered that a letter from Peter Smith reposed unread in her dressing-gown pocket, got out of the bath, and found a towel.

It was a short letter. She read it three times while she was dressed in a suitable evening gown by Dot.

'Peter says that he is well, and there has been no sign of pursuit from the anarchists,' she told Dot. Lovers came and lovers went in Phryne's house, but Peter the anarchist had been exceptional. The letter read:

> *Dearest Phryne,*
> *I love you with all my heart and I will never forget you. Do not forget me. You were like a vision, like water to a man dying of thirst. You saved me and the Revolution. Write to me. To lose you has taken sunlight out of my life.*
>
> > *Peter*

Phryne was suddenly and piercingly reminded of his touch, and a jolt ran down her spine.

'Did I pin you, Miss? Sorry. Keep still,' instructed Dot. Phryne stood still as ordered while Dot tweaked the flowing folds of the Érte dress, draped silk like a Greek maiden's, and found her sandals.

'There,' exclaimed Dot, standing beside Phryne in front of the pier-glass. 'Aren't we a pair?'

Phryne smiled. Dot glowed in the gold dress, Phryne shone white in the Érte. She blew a kiss to the reflection.

'We are beautiful,' she said lightly, patted Dot's cheek, and led the way down the stairs as the gong sounded to announce that dinner would shortly be served.

Bert and Cec were being served with beer in the parlour by Mr. Butler, who liked them both (having been a soldier himself), however much he might disapprove of their politics. Red-raggers, he had commented to Mrs. Butler in the privacy of her kitchen after first encountering Bert and Cec, but good chaps nonetheless. Mrs. Butler was pleased by their wholehearted appreciation of her cooking. No cook can ignore the opinion of a man who asks for three helpings. One is politeness, two is hunger, but three is a true and cherished compliment.

Thus Mrs. Butler had cooked Cec's favourite steak-and-kidney pudding, and had been in a ferment all afternoon in case it did not turn out of the dish in perfect unity.

Mr. Butler always absented himself on these occasions. He felt that the tension was not good for his health. Once he heard the 'ting' of the kitchen bell, indicating that the first course was ready to be served, he would return to his spouse without danger of being hit by a flying pan. Even the best cooks were saucepan throwers when the soufflé collapsed.

'Jeez, Cec, look!' Bert lifted his nose from his glass and grinned. Cec smiled his spaniel smile. Phryne and Dot entered the parlour with queenly grace and posed.

'Would you gentlemen like to escort us into dinner?' asked Phryne, and Bert abandoned his beer for the first time in his life. Phryne put a hand on his arm. Cec took Dot, walking carefully, awed in the presence of so much high fashion.

'You look bonzer, Miss,' said Cec slowly. 'I dunno where I ever seen you look so pretty. That cop, he's a lucky bloke.'

Dot blushed. Bert said, 'Yair, me and me mate are overwhelmed by your bee-yoo-ty. We ain't used to dining with two such visions of loveliness, eh Cec?'

'Too right.' Cec smiled down at Dot and she blushed again.

Mr. Butler replaced Bert's beer, since he disdained all wine as 'plonk,' as did Cec, though the latter admitted shyly to a taste for arak.

'Where on earth did you encounter arak?' asked Phryne as the soup was served; chicken bouillon. It was clear, hot, and just salty enough.

'In the war, Miss. We used to swap the Turks the medicinal brandy.'

'Of course, you two were at Gallipoli, weren't you? I expect that we have some arak. To me, it tastes like alcoholic aniseed balls, and one either likes aniseed, or one doesn't.'

'I don't like licorice or any of them things,' declared Bert, eating his soup rapidly but without spill or slurp.

'I used to love aniseed balls,' Dot confessed. 'I was the one who got the black jelly beans, but luckily, I liked them best.'

'You would have been useful at school, Dot, I used to give them to the gardener's dog. He seemed to like them.'

'How are the girls? Jane and my mate little Ruthie?' asked Bert. He had been instrumental in rescuing Ruth from domestic slavery, and her ambition to be a cook called to something deep in Bert, who had been hungry for a lot of his life.

'They are doing very well. I've been asked to go to the prize-giving at the end of the year; I believe Jane has won the mathematics prize. And Ruth has taken up swimming. Apart from not liking their music mistress they seem to be having a good time. Odd as it seems to have daughters, I'm glad I got them. They are such interesting children.'

The pudding was brought in, surrounded by vegetables—perfect, its crust unblemished by the slightest crack. Bert and Cec did not speak for some time, for one of Mrs. Butler's puddings was a masterpiece not to be slighted by conversation.

After an interval, Bert put down his fork and sighed. 'Every time I taste it I think that that was the best steak-and-kidney pud I've ever eaten,' he said. 'Our landlady has a good hand with the pastry, but Mrs. Butler keeps getting better.'

Mr. Butler memorized this, and filled Bert's glass again. When fruit and cheese were brought in, chairs were pushed back and cups of black coffee served. Mr. Butler searched his stock, and came back with pastis, which was close enough to arak. Dot accepted a glass, as did Cec, and Phryne chose port. Bert stuck to beer.

'Light up, gentlemen; I have a problem,' said Phryne.

'I thought you wasn't inviting us to dinner for the sake of our looks,' commented Bert, extracting tobacco pouch and papers from his pocket. 'For a dinner like that, however, I'm willing to talk about anything.'

'There is a man I am trying to find,' said Phryne slowly, 'who went off to the war looking like this.' She pushed the photograph of Victor Freeman across to Bert. He stared at it for a long moment, then passed it to Cec.

'Jeez, I was that young once,' said Bert. 'Eh, mate? I went off to fight looking like that. Stars in me eyes. Battle and heroics.' He licked the cigarette paper reflectively, paused, and groped for a match.

'He was at Gallipoli, was invalided home with shell-shock and a shrapnel wound on his head. After that, he changed. He couldn't stand noise. He quarrelled with his family; well, he quarrelled with his disgusting mother. Finally he left; he went out into the mountains to live alone, and he hasn't been heard of since 1920. Why did he go?'

Bert lit the cigarette and stared at the fireplace, where the maidenhair fern grew lush and green.

'We wouldn't tell this to just anybody, you know. But you're clever. You have to understand what it was like,' he said reluctantly. 'It was like hell. You gotta remember how young we were. I was eighteen, Cec was...how old were you, mate?'

'Seventeen,' said Cec.

'Yair. We joined up in a hurry, in case it was all over before we got there, and then kicked our heels for months in Cairo—of all the lousy cities in the world, Cairo is the lousiest. We was marched up and down and round till we could drill in our sleep. Cec and me hadn't met then. Come April 20th, we all get onto some old transports and then we get unloaded again. Wind got up. It got up me, too. Anyway, in the end we bucket across the sea and they tell us to land at this little cove. Now, it was a good idea, the Gallipoli campaign. If it had been done two months earlier and we had landed on the right beach the war woulda been three years shorter. But those bastards in Command sat around scratching until the Turks guessed and had time to prepare a little reception for us. We paddled ashore in rowboats and I was waist-deep in water when the gazumpers opened up—and rifle and machine-gun fire. The bullets skipped across the water, zip, zip, and the guns crashed, and the navy opened up behind us with shells, and I never heard such a noise in all my life, never. You didn't hear it, you felt it. It went through all your bones and made 'em quiver. I almost didn't care about getting hit. We struggled ashore and started to climb the cliffs—steep, scrubby cliffs—and up on top them damned machine-gunners, and snipers. The bloke ahead of me had his head blown off, clean as a whistle, and I'd never seen blood before, only in a street fight. Jeez, I was scared. But there was nowhere to go but up, so we went up, and by noon I reckon there was ten thousand men on them cliffs.

'After a while we dug in and the engineers started sapping. Two days we was under continuous fire and when they fell silent, them big guns, I thought I'd gone deaf. And we could hear the Turks yelling, "Allah! Il Allah Akhbar!" You remember, Cec?'

'Yair, mate, I remember.' Cec's eyes were dark with pain. 'We come up that first hill about two hours after you. By the time I got to cover all of me mates were gone. It was hot, too. Some bastard Johnny-sniper had holed me water bottle. I was perishing for a drink. And nothing but baking rocks, and the "ping" to remind yer not to raise yer head.'

'We got organized after a bit,' said Bert, butting out the cigarette and beginning on the manufacture of another. 'Got some rations and they brought these Indians and donkeys to bring water up from the tankers. Then it was just holding on. We scrounged a drink here and there, and they still thought we could take the ridge. We bloody tried. Then some clever bugger invented the periscope sight, so you could snipe without getting yer head blown off. But we died, my word we did. The dead lay between the lines, and swelled up in the heat, and stank. After a month the slightest scratch turned septic. And the big guns firing High Explosive, they never stopped, us or them. After a while you could tell what gun was firing by the sound. Them Turks could fight, too. "Allah!" they'd yell, and we'd scream, "Said baksheesh!" or, "Eggsacook!" like the wog traders said in Cairo, or, "Australia will be there!" And they'd reply, "Australia finish!" and we'd yell, "Diggers!" They were all right. They was caught in the same trap as us. Couple of times we organized truces to bury the bodies. And we'd swap, sometimes, our rum for that arak what tastes like petrol.'

'Did you see Simpson and his donkey?' asked Dot. Bert smiled.

'Yair. Murph and his Donk. Seen him walk the length of Hellfire Gully, down the sap, with a man on the donkey and another leaning on him. And Jacko Turk had two machine-guns fixed to fire the length of that gully, and the big guns was watering the ground with H.E. He copped it, though. Later. Most of us copped it.'

'Where did you meet Cec?' asked Phryne.

'Lone Pine,' said Cec. 'That's what Bert means about hell. Lots of blokes in Flanders whinged about the mud, said that hell was mud, deep enough to drown in. But hell ain't wet. Hell's a little tiny boiling-hot firing possy on a hill, where the grease from dead men drips on your head and you stink, and you scratch your skin off with lice, and big brown maggots drop in your face. I dreamed about them maggots for years. You couldn't eat because the blowies rushed into yer mouth as soon as you opened it. By then Bert's blokes was all gone, and there was only three men left in my company; we were palling up. I got sent up to Lone Pine and the first thing I saw was Bert's face, peering up over the edge, and a Turk sniper about to get him, so I shoved him down, and we was mates.'

Cec, unaccustomed to long speech, took a gulp of pastis.

'You got the sniper, too,' added Bert. 'Through his loophole. A bonzer shot. We'd sit up there for two days, breathing in that stench, and wishing we hadn't decided to be soldiers. Oh, dear Bill, what a bastard it was.'

'How did you get out?' asked Phryne. Bert looked indignant.

'Cec and me was originals. They let us go last, when they gave it up as a bad job. We set up the water-fired rifles and a few nice surprises for the first Turk that got into our trench. It was awful, leaving. Leaving all our mates behind, running like yeller dogs. I was walking around, setting up these rifles, and trying to explain to the mates we was abandoning that we wasn't running away, we was under orders. They tell me that it took two days before Johnny Turk dared to advance. We'da had him stonkered, if we'd started in time,' said Bert. 'They took us off to Cairo again—Jeez, I hate Cairo!—on a nice hospital ship, with sheets and blankets. Cec had enteric, and I had a bit of shrapnel in me knee, which had swelled up like billy-oh. We was pretty sorry for ourselves. But the navy was bonzer. They sat us on deck and scrubbed us raw with sea-water soap, and I never felt so clean. Then they gave us new clothes and stew with meat in and the first orange I'd seen since I left Melbourne. Then a nice nurse led me to a clean bed and I thought I'd died and gone to heaven. Eh, Cec?'

'I wasn't looking at the nurse,' said Cec, grinning, 'I was looking at the food. Cocoa so thick you could stand a spoon in it. Bread with real butter. Tea with milk. And the chats had gone. I was patterned all over with red dots from louse-bites.'

'Yair, they call them the Glories of War,' said Bert. 'So, we arrived in Cairo wearing badges of rank and blankets, and they put us in hospital again. But that ain't where your missing man got his shell-shock, not if he was with us. We were dead too quick to get shell-shock, I don't remember anyone getting it on Gallipoli. Musta been later.'

'Well, where did you go from there?'

'Flanders. Now, I reckon hell is wet. I didn't mind the heat or the flies—much. But that Flanders mud, slimy stinking corrupt mud with arms and legs and dead horses in it. I need another drink.'

Mr. Butler, whose military service had been in the Boer War, was so interested that he had forgotten to keep the glasses filled. He remedied this instantly.

'Yair, we was sent to...was it Marseilles, Cec?'

'Yair. Issued us with a tin hat and sent us out to the Bridioux salient. Near Armentières.'

'Yair, you're right. That was just before Pozières. We both got our tickets home at Pozières, and that's where your man would have got his shell-shock. Lots of us had it. July 20th. Worst shelling I ever been in—worse than Gallipoli, bigger guns, closer. Cec and me went over the top together and the machine-guns cut us all down. One bullet went straight through me chest, another through me thigh and into Cec's leg, another in the left arm. Cec dragged me back through the wire. I should have been a goner.'

'Least I could do, mate, after you kept the bullets off me,' said Cec laconically, and Bert laughed.

'I don't remember nothing about it until I was in a clearing station and the doctor was telling Cec, "I'm sorry, he's dead." Cec went blue and fell over me, and the doc thought he had two corpses on his hands. He got the shock of his life when I swore at him. They sent us back to England.'

'You remember what you said when we was in the ambulance?' asked Cec. Bert chuckled. 'He was lying there under about a ton of field dressings and he beckoned me to come closer and he said, "No fair, mate, those bastards are using live ammunition." I nearly laughed meself into another heart attack.'

'Yair, so they put us on a hospital ship. We stayed in London for a while until they said that me knee would always be dicky and I couldn't march on it, and that Cec had soldier's heart and might pop off any moment. Thanks a lot, you blokes, they said, you might as well go home. So we came home.'

'And Pozières?'

'Bad,' said Bert. 'We saw 'em come into the hospital, before they sent the poor bastards off to the loony bin. Barmy. Some of 'em were deaf, dumb or blind, though they didn't have a scratch. Some of 'em had visions. The shell-shock blokes couldn't stand noise. They'd go off pop if they heard a truck backfire. But your bloke'd be all right out in the bush, there ain't much noise bar the odd thunderstorm. If he was alive after the war then chances are he's still alive. Well, that was the Great War. Roll up, roll up, and get your block knocked off. But we won,' said Bert. 'Australia will be there. Even if it was a capitalist plot, which it was. Eh, Cec?'

'I still feel bad about it,' said Cec softly. 'Leaving them there. Our mates. On that damned cliff.'

'Yair,' agreed Bert. He drank his beer in silence.

'Let us talk about something more cheerful,' suggested Phryne. 'How is the taxi business?'

'Good,' said Cec. 'Since the waterfront is still on strike we've been working double shifts. The clients like the bonzer new cab.'

Later, as Phryne farewelled her guests at the door, Bert was struck by a sudden thought.

'You be careful,' he said seriously. 'Them shell-shock patients could turn very nasty. And strong! If you need to find him, maybe you'd better take a gun.'

'To defend myself?'

'To put the poor bugger out of his misery. Beg pardon. Padre always told me me language was sulphurous. But you shoulda heard him when he fell in a shell-hole! 'Night, thanks for dinner.' Bert and Cec left.

Phryne, shaken with horrible images, called for more port and sat down again by the fire.

Dot hung up the sunrise dress on her door, where she could see it from her bed, and fell asleep. Dot's father and two uncles had been in the Great War. She had heard it all before.

Chapter Seven

FLORENCE: It's not my fault.

NICKY: Of course it's your fault, Mother, who else's fault could it be?

The Vortex, Noel Coward

The doorbell pealed. Phryne looked at her watch. Eleven o'clock. 'Charles!' she exclaimed.

Mr. Butler admitted a trembling figure and supplied it with a drink.

'Charles, there you are at last!' Phryne saw that Charles had not borne stress well. His normally pink face was white. At some time he had bitten his lip hard enough to draw blood, and his mouth looked swollen and bee-stung. As he put out a hand she noticed that all his fingernails had been gnawed to the quick.

'You said that I had to come,' he faltered. 'So here I am. I suppose they are going to lock me up?'

'Yes, Charles, for a while. But only until I can find out who really did it. Have another drink and we shall talk. Where have you been?'

'I spent the first night at a hotel. Then, you won't believe this, Phryne, but Ben Rodgers has been hiding me.'

'Ben Rodgers? But you tried to steal his girl! Why should Ben hide you?'

'I don't know.' Charles drained the brandy and soda and held out his glass for another. 'He's making arrangements to get me onto a ship, he's been really helpful. Only a week ago he was threatening to kill me and I thought he meant it. I was scared to death of him. Then he passed the word around that he was willing to help and came and got me from the hotel. I've been in his flat. The police had already searched it, you see. I explained about Nerine. The stupid tart had told Ben that I was trying to seduce her. He's fiendishly jealous. When I explained what I wanted of her, Ben became quite polite. Said he had mistaken my intentions. Also said that Nerine wouldn't leave his band, which is true. Of course, he despises me. But he's been very good. If you hadn't persuaded me to give myself up I would have been on a cargo carrier to New Zealand tonight.'

'I spoke to Bobby,' said Phryne, still puzzled by Charles. Every time she spoke to him his character seemed to flicker.

'And you said that Vic was alive.'

'Yes. Or he was alive, until 1920. He was in Gippsland. He came back from the war shell-shocked. I don't know how long he was in Melbourne before he went bush.'

'Oh, I can tell you how long. About six months. I have always wondered about that interval. My mother kept me away from home for six months in the spring and summer of 1916. That was when she told me that Victor had died. And she never stopped taunting me with him. Vic was brave, I was not—and I'm not. Vic was clever, and I'm not—that's right again. The only thing I had that Vic didn't have, apart from being alive, was the business. I'm good at business. My factory makes very good blankets. But blankets are not glory. I suffered because of Vic. And my mother knew that he was alive all that time, the bitch. The conniving old bitch! How could she do that to me?'

'A good question, to which I don't know the answer. But there is a further complication. Your father's will left you the business, and the house and the money to Victor. He never got around to changing it, apparently, or perhaps he knew that Vic was still with us. So Vic must be found, or proved dead. Do you see?'

Charles saw. He tossed down his drink and held out the glass for yet another refill, fizzing with outrage.

'So it's not enough that I'm to be accused of a murder I didn't commit, but Victor must turn up and steal my inheritance! It's too much! Why does everything always happen to me? Why didn't he have the grace to die like a hero?'

'Charles dear, do stop asking unanswerable questions and pay attention. What about the murder of Bernard? Did you know him?'

'Yes.'

'And you knew that he had incriminating photographs of you?'

'Yes.' Charles took a cigarette from the box on the table and lit it with a jazz-striped lighter.

'And you were at the Green Mill to watch him take part in that ghastly dance marathon?'

'Yes. Mother was nagging at me to go out with you and I thought that as long as I had to go, I might as well see Bernard in the marathon and watch him break a leg, with any luck. But I never have any luck. If someone was going to kill him, and there must have been hundreds of people who wanted him dead as much as I did, why did they have to choose the night I was there? It looks bad, doesn't it?'

'Yes. But there are points in your favour. One is the fact that you faint at the sight of blood. The other is the weapon. It still hasn't been found.'

'Did they search all those musicians?'

'Yes.'

'Because they were all over the body like a rash. Tintagel Stone and Ben.'

'Yes, but neither had any reason to kill Bernard. Also, they only came down to see what had happened after he fell, and he was dead when he hit the ground.'

'They'll hang me, won't they? The hangman will come up in a mask and put a bag over my head and a noose around my neck and they'll kill me, they'll kill me!'

Charles' voice had risen to a scream. Phryne slapped him, hard, across the cheek. He gaped at her.

'You hit me!' he gasped. 'You *hit* me!'

'And I will hit you again if you don't pipe down. You'll rouse the house. You have overlooked the factor that is going to preserve your miserable life.'

'What?' asked Charles, hand still cupping his reddened cheek.

'Me,' said Phryne immodestly. 'I am a vital factor. I will find out what happened and I will get you out.'

Phryne found a gasper and Charles leaned forward to light it.

'That's a pretty lighter, I've not seen one similar.'

'Ben made it. He used to be a jeweller. Makes rings and jazz bracelets as well, though not the sort of stuff you'd wear. Nerine likes gold. He gave it to me, I lost mine.'

'Does Ben know that you are giving yourself up?'

'No, well, he wasn't there, so I left him a note.'

'I see. Well, I'll just call the cops and get you safely into a nice quiet cell for the night. Now don't worry, Charles. I will find out who did it and then they will release you.'

'You promise?'

'I promise.'

Charles, watery around the eyes but bearing up reasonably well, was taken away half an hour later by a polite but very large sergeant, who agreed that the prisoner should be lodged alone and that Miss Fisher and his family could visit him in the morning. Phryne watched him go with mixed emotions. Who on earth *had* killed the unfortunate and scarcely missed Bernard?

A taxi screeched to a halt, narrowly missing the van which was taking the prisoner away. Ben Rodgers leapt out, scarlet with fury, and raced up the steps.

'Where's Charles? Have you got him?'

'No,' Phryne replied, moving back a little and getting a grip on the neck of the vase which stood by the door. 'The police have him. He has given himself up. He didn't do it.'

'How do you know?' snarled the trumpeter. 'He had reason.'

'Reason, but no means. And I shall prove it,' she added, securing the vase in case this brass player lived up to his billing.

'You will?' he sneered.

Phryne smiled. 'I will,' she said confidently. Ben Rodgers glared his best hundred-watt glare at her, spat at her feet, and ran down the steps again. Only once he was safely in his taxi and gone did Phryne close the door.

'That being so, I shall put myself to bed. Pity there's no one in it but me, but there it is.'

Suppressing a pang for the loss of Peter Smith, most passionate of anarchists, she obeyed her own order and was soon asleep.

In the early morning she dreamt about the roses again. A black, shiny snail slithered into the heart of them. Phryne woke, told herself firmly that it was her subconscious trying to tell her something, and went back to sleep to give it another chance.

It appeared to have shot its bolt, however, and she woke at the usual time unenlightened and with the knowledge that she was going to have to visit Mrs. Freeman again. This did not improve an already depressing day. The skies wept.

'Bother, bother, bother!' exclaimed Dot, as Phryne's shoelace broke in her hands. 'It is not going to be a good day, Miss.'

'I agree. Charles Freeman is in the hands of the cops and I'm going to have to see his revolting mother again to get more information about Victor. Have the photographs come from Jack Robinson?'

'Yes, Miss.' Dot tugged at a second lace and it also broke.

'Perhaps I'll wear another pair of shoes, Dot,' said Phryne gently. 'I don't seem to be getting on with inanimate objects today. I'll do a sweep; Mrs. F and Bobby. One of them will be pleased to see me.'

Bobby answered the door in his dressing-gown.

'I've got a present for you,' said Phryne, and he snatched at the packet of photographs, clutching them to his bosom.

'Thank you, Miss Fisher, how can I ever thank you? Since I spoke to you, I feel free of Charles. He's lost his hold over me.

I can't invite you in. I…er…have company. Perhaps you'll dine with me tonight?'

'I have an engagement,' Phryne said, smiled, and walked out of his life.

'Dot was right,' she said to herself as she turned the car. 'It is not going to be a good day. But if I've missed the gratitude I've also missed being wept over again. Ah well. Ho for Mrs. Freeman.' At least it had stopped raining.

Mrs. Freeman, it appeared, had not moved since Phryne had last seen her. She was still lying on the couch with a maid in attendance and still weeping. She might not have a heart, thought Phryne, but her tear-ducts worked overtime.

'Miss Fisher, they have arrested my son!'

'Which one?' asked Phryne nastily, sitting down on the edge of the couch. 'Enough hysterics, Mrs. Freeman, you weary me and you do not impress me. A woman with a heart as hard as yours should not shriek. It does not convince. Charles will be freed as soon as I solve the murder. Now, do you want me to continue to try to find your other, shamefully neglected, son—or would you like me to resign the case? There are two other lady detectives practising in Melbourne, and they would be pleased to take up the search.'

Mrs. Freeman was silent for a moment. Phryne wondered whether she was gathering strength to have her impudent visitor flung out of the house, but she spoke quietly.

'Please continue. I do not know why I trust you, Miss Fisher, for you are the rudest young woman I have ever had the misfortune to encounter, but I do.'

'Very well. Have you any clue as to where Victor might be? When did he return to Melbourne, where from, and with what injuries?'

'He was sent home from England in September 1916. He had been in Lady Montague's Rest Hospital but they said that he could not be cured. He was blind for three months, apparently. After Gallipoli he was at a place in France that they made a song about. What was it…?' She began to hum, and then to sing softly in a dry, tuneless soprano, 'Mademoiselle from Armentières, that was it. A battle at a place called Pozières.'

So Bert was right, thought Phryne, that was where poor Victor had lost his marbles. Pozières. 'Lots of us copped it,' Bert had said.

'Then there was a terrible dilemma, you see. He was, well, he was nervy and jumpy and rude and couldn't sleep. I could not let poor Charles see his heroic brother reduced to screaming like a fishwife. He really was impossible, Miss Fisher. And he'd been such a quiet boy, fond of music and riding. So I told Charles that Victor was dead. That solicitor chap has been most impudent about it. He said that to say someone is dead when you know they're not is fraud, and that I was trying to make him commit a fraud on the Supreme Court. I wouldn't think of such a thing. Anyway, Victor's been missing for eight years. He can be declared dead. The solicitor had the nerve to tell me I shouldn't look for Victor if I want to put in an application for that. But then if Victor is declared dead and didn't ever marry, and I'm sure he didn't, then the other part of the property doesn't go to Charles, it goes into—what was the word?—residue, that's it. And my stupid husband left the residue of his estate to the Royal Children's Hospital. It means I don't get anything but my jewellery and the clothes I stand up in!'

Some reason for the hysteria was now apparent.

'But if you find that Victor is really dead, the house comes to me, because he made an army will which left me all his property, the dear boy.'

Phryne was nauseated, but had to keep listening.

'Anyway,' said Mrs. Freeman, dragging herself away from the iniquities of the law, 'Victor was so difficult that I moved out while he was in the house. My husband always did indulge him. I was staying at the Brighton Hotel when I got a telegram saying that I could return. When I got home my husband told me that Victor had decided to go into the bush, where it was quiet, because he couldn't bear noise. He'd been gone a whole day, never even said goodbye to me. I was so hurt. His own mother! How could he just go off like that, leave me without a word? I never knew where he went, and I never heard from him again. My husband sent a cheque every year to a place called Talbotville, in Gippsland somewhere. But he never said, he never told me, that he had heard from Victor. After I spoke with you the other day I searched my husband's desk; all the legal papers were gone, of course, but I found this. And I never even suspected.'

She produced a bundle of letters, tied with tape. They had been read and reread and then lovingly folded into their original creases and stacked in order of receipt.

'Wicked man!' Mrs. Freeman fanned herself vigorously. 'I never knew that Victor wrote to him. He never replied to me. And I wrote to him every year!'

'Can I take these?' asked Phryne. 'Have you read them?'

'No. Well, only the first one. He says such things—I couldn't bear to read any more. Take them with pleasure.'

Phryne, who did not feel that she could bear much more of Mrs. Freeman's company, stood up, tucking the bundle of letters into her bag.

'And you will get Charles for me, you will get him back?' the woman pleaded, snatching Phryne's hand.

Phryne detached herself, agreed that she would restore Charles as soon as she could, and left.

In the park Phryne stopped to watch children playing with an airgun. It was probable that airguns, like dancing, singing, bicycle riding, ball games, and any other form of amusement which might appear dangerous to the local government, were banned in the park. Phryne hoped they would not be caught. Pfft! went the gun, itching at her memory. There were four children: a plump, bossy, blonde one; a thin dark one; a strong-willed girl with chestnut hair; and a small, freckled red-headed kid. They quarrelled as though it was their standard method of communication.

'My shot! My shot!' bellowed the small boy as his dark-haired sister snatched the rifle. Despite pulling her face into a fearful grimace, closing both eyes, and aiming the barrel with wobbling hands, she was by far the best shot.

'Pfft!'

'Oh, well done!' said the plump blonde. 'Bull's-eye! I don't know why you can shoot better than all the rest of us,' she commented, taking the gun away and giving it to the small girl. 'You're not supposed to close both eyes, you know. How can you see the target? Your turn, Anne.' The small girl butted the gun firmly against a strong shoulder, aimed with care, and hit the edge of the target.

'It fluttered,' she complained. Phryne sighted a keeper looming through the trees.

'Run, kids, it's the keeper,' she called, and they gathered up the gun, a fallen sunhat, and the paper target, and ran for their lives.

Phryne started the Hispano-Suiza and went home for a soothing lunch and a read of Victor's letters.

Tintagel Stone had rung to invite Phryne to another jazz club; she left word that she accepted.

Lunch was a grilled whiting with salad and boiled new potatoes, a Charlotte Russe, and several cups of strong coffee. There was something wrong, she realized, either with Mrs. Freeman's legal advisor, or the way she had interpreted his advice. It would make no difference to Victor's inheritance if he were presumed dead or really dead. But the law being such a minefield, Phryne rang Jilly at her office to check. She hoped that Jilly had forgiven her for losing her the big murder trial in which she had been convinced she would make her mark.

'Phryne, how delightful to hear your voice. Sorry to hurry you, old girl, but I've got a bail coming on at Russell Street in an hour and I'm not only making bricks without straw, but without mud, mortar, and water, as well. What can I do for you?'

Phryne explained her problem.

'No, she must have misheard the solicitor. There's no difference between being presumed dead and being dead. I mean, no difference in law. I suppose there is a difference if you are still alive on a desert island somewhere and the Crown is giving your estate away.'

'So, in terms of inheritance, you might as well be presumed dead as dead?'

'Exactly so, dear Phryne. Now if there's nothing else I really must go. I just can't imagine how I'm going to get this client out of the watch-house, I really can't.'

Jilly rang off. Phryne took her coffee and the letters to her own sitting room on the first floor. The house was quiet. Mr. and Mrs. Butler were having their afternoon rest. Dot was out visiting her sister, who had just had her first baby. The letters made a loud crackle as Phryne carefully unfolded them.

There were eight in total, all written in a laborious but educated hand, in very black ink on ordinary stationer's paper. They were very neat; not a blot or a splatter on any of them. Victor had not gone so far as to give any permanent address.

The first letter was postmarked 'Dargo' and was dated 29th March 1917. It was headed 'Railway Hotel, Bairnsdale' and read:

Dear Dad,

I got here all right. I'm going to have to go right out into the bush to find some quiet. It's too noisy even here. There's a bloke taking stores to Dargo. He says I can go with him. I think I'll do that. Still can't sleep. I'm sorry I couldn't stay at home, Dad. Mum never let up nagging me, and screaming and fainting, and I couldn't stand it. Even when she left, I still felt like she'd come back any minute. I'll let you know when I stop somewhere.

Vic

The next was headed 'Commercial Hotel, Dargo,' dated 15th April 1917.

Dear Dad,

Thanks for the cheque. I can't get out into the real mountains this late, the snowline is coming down, but

I'm going out to a place called Talbotville, where there is
a post office, and I can take a packhorse further. Still can't
sleep, but there's a lot worse off than me.

Vic

The next one was addressed from 'The Pub, Talbotville' and
read:

Dear Dad,

I really like this place, it's so small. The local blokes
were a bit stand-offish till they gave me a mean devil of
a stockhorse to ride and I stuck on good-o. I've been out
on a long ride with pack-horses to deliver stores to the
outliers up on the high plains; all sorts of things, tins and
even a stove! And a cross-cut saw! You can imagine how
the neddy took to that! I think I'll stay here.

Vic

There had been a long gap before the fourth letter. As Phryne
unfolded it a small pressed flower, which might have originally
been pink, fell out. It had a faint scent of eucalypt. 'MacAlister
Springs' was the superscription.

Dear Dad,

Thanks for the cheque. I'm sorry it's been so long since
I wrote. As soon as the snow retreated, I bought a tent
and some gear from Dargo and went wandering. It's so
quiet here. The mountains are grand. I sleep like a log. I
can't believe it's been a year since I came home. I'm much
better. The leaseholder says I can stay here as long as I don't
start a business, and there's no fear of that. Charlie is the
businessman. I got a letter from Mum and she says she's
told Charlie I'm dead. Perhaps it's better. I've got a dog
and a horse and all the silence in the world. I'm learning
how to build a slab hut.

Vic

Phryne drank her coffee thoughtfully. She had never been out into the real bush, only on Church picnics to the wilds of Werribee as a small child, before she went to England. She wondered what solace a shell-shocked boy, living skin-to-lousy-skin with other humans for years, would find in high mountains and silence and loneliness. Phryne decided that she was too gregarious to stand it.

'MacAlister Springs,' read the next, dated 2nd December 1918.

> Dear Dad,
>
> They tell me in Talbotville it's all over. The Great War, I mean. I can't feel any triumph, only relief, and regret for all my mates that didn't come home. We left them, Dad, on that cliff at Gallipoli and in the mud at Pozières. I was lucky, compared to them. I've got a horse (Lucky) and a dog (Mack). I finished my hut for last winter. If I run out of meat there's plenty of bunnies. I found a blackbird with a broken wing and he's staying too, and I share my breakfast with the kookaburras. At mustering time I help with the strayed beasts. Don't keep asking me to come back, Dad. I'm happy. I couldn't stand Mum and the city again. Besides, I'm dead.
>
> Vic

Letter number five was dated 11th November 1919 and just said:

> I got the cheque, Dad. I can't help remembering them. One of the boys at Talbotville asked me what it was like. I couldn't tell him. It was a bad winter. Can you send me a parcel of books? Not adventures. My own books from when I was a kid; The Wind in the Willows, and Treasure Island and all those. I can order the others from Melbourne.

There were still three letters left, and Phryne had been told that Victor had not been heard of since 1920. The sixth was dated 26th September 1920 and said:

Dear Dad,

I'm onto a bit of work here, so you don't need to send any more money. I can't come home, Dad. Here is my home. I would miss the great silence too much. Thanks for the books. They arrived all in order.

Vic

Number seven included another flower. The faded yellow petals crackled, although Phryne handled it as gently as she could. It was headed 'MacAlister Springs' and dated 12th January 1921.

Dear Dad,

Happy new year. I'm getting on bonzer. Thanks for the chocolates and biscuits and stuff. I can get rough supplies from Talbotville but the shop doesn't go as far as chocolates! Thanks. I can't come home, Dad, really. I can't. This year the forest is as dry as a chip, and we are all watching for the smoke.

Vic

The final letter had no heading, just a date: 9th October 1924. It began hastily.

Dear Dad,

Please stop asking me to come back. I haven't got a job in the city. Mum has declared me dead. What would Charlie think if I suddenly turned up? And I'm not used to society now, Dad. I won't write again. Thanks for everything, Dad.

This one had a parting salutation:

Your loving son,
Vic

Phryne carefully folded all the letters and retied the bundle. The house was quite silent. Phryne had the immediate urge to put on the wireless, to sing, to move. She did not like silence. The noise of cities, the passing of feet and cars, voices calling and laughing, dogs barking, soothed and amused her. Would it be right to go seeking this damaged young man, who at the age of nineteen had wandered off into that vast space, and try to drag him back to this noisy place just because of the testatory fears of a neurotic mother?

Phryne remembered, with a sudden chill, that Mrs. Freeman didn't want Victor back. She wanted him dead.

Chapter Eight

You don't like my peaches,
why do you shake my tree?
You don't like my peaches,
why do you shake my tree?

'St. Louis Blues,' W. C. Handy

Phryne was dressing for her outing with Tintagel Stone when her necklace of jet beads broke. She and Dot dived to the floor to gather them all before they should roll out of sight under the furniture, to be vacuumed up by Mr. Butler and his new machine. Phryne poured her beads into a stocking, and Dot came to add hers, cupped in a red silk scarf which had also been on the floor.

As Dot held out her hand, with the black bead nestling in the centre of the red silk, Phryne at last caught the memory that had been eluding her for days. The picture stood still in her mind's eye and allowed her to focus on it. The snail in the centre of the red roses. The black bead in Dot's red palm. The knife still in the wound of the dead man at the Green Mill, the odd round haft of the knife in Bernard Stevens' chest. The blot of bright blood had made an irregular splotch, about the size of a hand, and in the middle was the knife.

It had been there when the man had fallen; Phryne had seen it. It had not been there after the members of Tintagel's Jazz Makers had finished their examination of the corpse. In that interval, someone had removed the murder weapon, then somehow smuggled it out of the Green Mill without being caught. How? That was another problem. The relief of catching the memory was profound.

'Miss, Miss, are you all right?' asked Dot, worried by her silence and air of abstraction. 'It can be fixed, Miss. We've got all the beads. And you can wear the other one.'

'It's all right, Dot, dear, the necklace doesn't matter in the slightest. I have been trying to remember something and it just came back when I saw you holding that bead. And thank God, I thought I was losing my reason. But I had only mislaid it,' she said, and chuckled. 'Well, well! I shall have to think about this.'

Dot was looping the stocking carefully, so that it would not be damaged by the beads.

'And I shall have a very interesting evening. Now, have I got everything? Cigarettes? No, Dot, I'll take the bigger bag.'

'It doesn't match so well,' observed Dot, picking up a pouchy black velvet bag and putting down a flat beaded clutch-purse.

'I know, but I need to carry more things than that little one will hold.'

Before Dot's censorious gaze, Phryne loaded the black bag with her little gun, a wodge of banknotes, a handkerchief, some cigarettes, a lighter, and a lipstick.

'Miss, you're expecting trouble,' she chided. 'Are you going alone? Why not take Mr. Bert and Mr. Cec?'

'They wouldn't fit in. I'll be all right, Dot, I assure you.'

Phryne hugged Dot impatiently.

'Now don't get all sniffy, Dot dear, I tell you I shall be all right. Perfectly safe,' said Phryne, and she breezed down to meet her escort, who had been waiting in the salon for twenty minutes.

Phryne made an entrance that was worth waiting for. She was wearing a black silk dress, dance-length, which glittered with silver beads in the pattern of constellations; silver stockings and black shoes. On her head was a silver cap, beaded with the zodiac around its flat brim. Long, delicate strings of beads trailed around her enigmatic face and stopped just short of her neck. 'Oh, Phryne,' said Tintagel Stone, eyes alight. 'Magnificent!' She walked into his embrace.

'Are you fond of the stars?' she asked lightly.

'I have always reached for them,' he replied, sliding a hand down over the Southern Cross. Phryne pushed him gently away.

'We are going out,' she said, and Tintagel released her reluctantly.

'If you insist,' he agreed. 'We are playing at the Jazz Club, and Nerine has agreed to sing. I don't know what you did to her, but it has had an excellent effect. Did you find her husband?'

'Yes. He's dead,' said Phryne, preceding him down the hall. 'I started from the premise that anyone who had Nerine would not willingly have let her go. She has…appeal.'

'Yes.' Tintagel Stone opened the car door and climbed in. 'You could say that. Raw, naked passion is more like it.'

'And has she never attracted you?' Phryne started the engine.

'Me?' Tintagel's mouth dropped open. 'Are you quite mad? She's been with Ben Rodgers ever since I met her, and you know…'

'What trumpeters are. Yes,' sighed Phryne, 'I know. Has he always been that jealous?'

'Yes. Threw one patron down the steps at a nightclub, we never played there again. Big bloke, too, but that doesn't matter to Ben, not when he's in a rage. And he'll wait, too, he's as patient as a cat and has all the delicacy and refinement of a great white shark. Not a nice man, perhaps, but a bloody great trumpeter. Mind you, even for a trumpeter he's a bit extreme.'

'You would go so far as to say that?' marvelled Phryne. 'Is he capable of murder?'

'Phryne, are you saying…what are you saying?'

'Just answer the question.'

'Yes, he is capable of murder. Look, are you suggesting that Ben killed that Bernard chap? He didn't know him! He had no reason to kill him! And anyway, he was right in front of me when the fellow collapsed. I swear that he was never off the bandstand, not until the chap was dead and on the floor.'

'Tintagel, I fear that you have not been wholly frank with me,' said Phryne severely. 'Not frank at all. Not what one would expect of a Cornishman. If you didn't think Ben had something to do with this, why did you smuggle the murder weapon out of the Green Mill?'

'Me?'

'That's very good,' said Phryne, approving of his blank innocence. 'That tone must be very useful in nasty situations. I'm sure it has convinced many a suspicious cop.'

'But not you?' His voice was level, containing an undercurrent of stress; perhaps anger, perhaps amusement.

'No, not me,' agreed Phryne. 'Doubtless you washed your shirt-cuff as soon as you got home, but you forgot the crust of blood on the inside of the suit-sleeve, caused by pushing a bloody knife up there when you thought no one was watching.'

'How did you know about the blood?' The voice was still calm.

'I felt for it when I hugged you, just now.'

'You are the most…' He struggled for words. 'The most…'

'The usual phrase is cold-hearted, devious bitch,' supplied Phryne helpfully, pulling the car into the kerb and stopping. She turned to face Tintagel and did not smile.

'Marvellous girl!' exploded Tintagel, staring with open admiration into her green eyes. 'I thought no one had noticed.'

'Quite. Once I worked that out, I wondered why you should hide the murder weapon, unless it would point straight to someone you felt the need to protect. Now it couldn't be Iris, she never moved; nor could it be you. I knew where you were.' Her voice was reminiscent and warm. 'I could see you. You had no connection with the dance marathon, and in any case the dancers couldn't reach, I was in the way. So he had to be killed from a distance. Come on. You'll be late.'

Tintagel Stone, emotions in ferment, was nevertheless a professional performer. He entered the Jazz Club at a run and found the Jazz Makers already there.

He collected his banjo and stepped onto the stage, where Nerine waited in a black dress with a sparkly pink overlay of chiffon, cut low enough to reveal breasts which, although definitely out of fashion, were smooth, marmoreal, and perfect. Both Nerine and Ben Rodgers gave Phryne a narrowed glance, Nerine squinting to sight her even at three yards.

'Tintagel Stone and the Jazz Makers,' announced the MC. 'The band that made St. Vitus dance!'

They launched into a fast, slightly discordant version of 'Tiger Rag,' which had become their trademark. Over the melody the cornet wailed, muted and skilled, never quite entirely out of key.

'I hate to see that evening sun go down,' sang Nerine, who appeared to have the St. Louis blues. 'I hate to see that evening sun go down, because my baby he done gone and left this town.' As always, her potent appeal made itself felt. The crowded club was quiet and intent. Over near the kitchen door, a ferocious argument about the True Meaning of Jazz died down to a murmur.

'St. Louis woman, love her diamond ring,' sang Nerine, huskily but with great force. 'Drag that man around by her apron string.' Then came a wail which should have been ridiculous but was heart-rending. 'If it weren't for her powder and store-bought hair, that man I love wouldn't have gone nowhere.'

Phryne sat down at a table in the front, against stiff opposition from a number of gentlemen who wanted to get as close to Nerine as they could. 'If you don't like my peaches,' she sang, hand on hips, swaying slightly, 'why do you shake my tree?' A shiver ran through the club. The red hair shadowed her breast as she shook her head. 'If you don't like my peaches, why do you shake my tree?' The head came up, the hips forward, and the dress shifted and gaped. Even Phryne, who was not attracted to women, was not unmoved. 'You get out of my orchard, and let my peach tree be!' The singer knew what effect she was producing in this predominantly male environment, even relished it. The red lips curved over white teeth as she smiled into the dark. Phryne, for the first time since she had been fourteen, felt small, pale, and flat-chested, devoid of charm in the face of this arrogant and voluptuous challenge. She shook herself and ordered coffee.

The band swung into a fast 'Basin Street Blues.' Phryne drank her coffee and recovered her self-confidence.

I could demand an explanation, she thought, as the trumpet, expertly handled, wailed and clucked. I could break up the feast with much admired disorder. I know that Tintagel is covering up for someone. But I like Tintagel. There isn't any real need to do anything. Jack Robinson will work out in a couple of days that it wasn't Charles, and will let him go. Who cares who killed Bernard Stevens, anyway? He was a blackmailer. Charles is an unattractive character too, flirting with poor Bobby and leading him on. I don't like either of them, so why am I interfering?

She was served with more coffee, paid for it, then was possessed of a sudden disgust for her own ways.

She sipped the coffee, which was as weak as dishwater. Maybe I'll go and look for the errant son. I'll ring up this Talbotville place, anyway. I need cold, and silence. What was it he called it? The great silence. There's too much noise in here and I don't like myself at all at the moment, or the game that I am playing.

Leaving the coffee half drunk, she got up decisively and went out. The door swung shut behind the flicker of her constellations.

Chapter Nine

Away! Away! For I will fly to thee
'Ode to a Nightingale,' John Keats

Phryne slept the night without dreaming, and the next morning took up the packet of letters from Victor to his father. She read them again, then looked at the photograph, which Dot had placed on her bedside table. Not a pretty face, but, as Dot had said, one you could trust. His letters were painfully honest, and his father's importunities doubly selfish. She began to think that Mrs. Freeman and her spouse had deserved each other. She was as self-centred as a compass. So was Charles, always wailing, 'Why should this happen to me? How could anyone do this to me?' in that distressing way. Phryne did not like questions without an answer, and the only answer to those questions was, 'Why not?' which was not satisfactory, however true. Poor Victor, recovering his balance in the cold silence, happy with his mountains, nagged by his father to return when there was nothing for him in the city. His mother disliked him, his brother thought he was dead, and he had said himself that he was no good at business. His father can only have wanted him back to be his companion, or possibly as a pawn in a power struggle with his wife. Charles did not even know that Victor was alive.

How thoughtless, to continually demand Victor's return! Why did his father not go and visit him, or meet him in one of these towns with outlandish names, Talbotville or Dargo, instead of writing to require the boy's presence?

Perhaps he had visited. Phryne wondered as to who would know. Mr. Freeman did not seem to have been a confiding man. Mrs. Freeman had not even known that he had corresponded with Victor.

Phryne went down to the hall and obtained an operator, who connected her after considerable delay to the post office in Talbotville.

'Yair?' a strong, confident man's voice said.

'I want to speak to Victor Freeman.'

'To Vic? He ain't...' the voice changed suddenly. 'I ain't heard of no one of that name.'

'You have, you know.' Phryne was nettled. 'I don't mean him any harm but I need to talk to Victor Freeman.'

'No one here of that name,' snarled the voice, and the line went dead.

A mystery, Phryne thought, suddenly angry. What had been going on in Talbotville? Well, she would find out. Phryne did not like being cut off when she was inquiring with the best of motives. As soon as I can find some suitable maps, she resolved, I shall take the Moth up, and fly to wherever the place is, and look for Victor. And if I find him and he wants to stay unfound, then I shall leave him alone.

Bunji Ross, in the mess room of the Sky High Flying School, Essendon (Prop. W. McNaughton), spread out the maps and made a grimace.

'It's very lumpy country, Phryne,' she commented. 'It's the highest country in Australia, mountains extending into the Great Divide and up to the Snowy. I'd call it inaccessible and I can see why you want to fly it, but...'

Phryne surveyed Bunji with affection. From a track rider of race horses she had become a very good pilot of aeroplanes. Bunji was small and plump, with permanently ink-stained fingers, and brown hair cropped mercilessly close because it impeded her flying helmet. Phryne and Bunji had been at school together, where Bunji had got her name from her endless and inventive uses for indiarubber. She had been a dead shot with an ink-dart.

'You are taking the Moth?' Phryne nodded. 'Well, let's have a look at the route. These maps are the best they had; I believe that a new survey is planned, but these were made by the original surveyor back in 1856. The topography won't have changed all that much, I suppose. Now, you leave from here and fly to—what is the name of the town?'

'Talbotville.'

'Aha. Here it is. In that big river valley, there. That looks like a possible landing, though if it is all forested you may have a little difficulty getting out again.'

'Then to…' Phryne consulted the letters. 'MacAlister Springs.'

'Pour me some more tea, will you, Phryne? I can't see a MacAlister Springs, but there is a MacAlister River. Here. It seems to rise in the shadow of this big 'un, Mount Howitt. That valley, old girl, is not passable. Look at the contours!'

Phryne gazed at the map. Two rivers rose from the bulk of Mount Howitt; the Wonnangatta, flowing east around the mountain, and the MacAlister, flowing south-west. Bunji was right. There did not look to be a flat space at all inside the valley of the MacAlister, and the contours of the mountains connected to Mount Howitt were perpendicular.

'I've borrowed this from the walking club,' said Bunji, laying another map on the table. 'It's a walker's map. It names all those peaks. See, here, from Mount Howitt. You are going to love the names, Phryne.' Her blunt forefinger traced the spiky lines. 'Between Howitt and the next one is the Cross-Cut Saw, and where the Wonnangatta River rises is the Terrible Hollow. It looks like a long way down. Then there is Mount Speculation, and on the other side of the river, the Viking. It appears that the bit of high plain next to Mount Howitt is the Howitt Plains, which leads onto the Snowy Plains. Now, I've only seen heights like this in the Himalayas. Big mountains, and they cause a lot of flying problems. Downdrafts that can drop you five hundred feet in a second. Mist. Cloud. You know about cloud. You can be tootling along without a care when the cloud lifts and you're head-on into a cliff. I don't think this is a good idea, Phryne, my dear. Isn't there another way to get to this dratted place?'

'Packhorse and days and days,' commented Phryne. 'I'm in a hurry.'

'You don't want to be in so much of a hurry that you arrive dead,' argued Bunji. 'However, if you insist. Well, you can get to Talbotville all right; it's in the basin of that big river, the Wongungurra, and it seems to be at least half a mile wide around there. Your best bet for the MacAlister Springs place might be to drop down onto the Howitt Plains. Aha, yes, there it is—the Springs. From Talbotville, assuming that you can get aloft, it's not a great distance. You can carry enough fuel to get to these springs, provided you keep between the two rivers and fly toward Mount Howitt. Yes. Take off west from Talbotville, over Mount Cynthia, follow the Snowy Plains straight for Mount Howitt, and land just before the mountain. The walking club says that it is virgin forest and very thick in the valleys, but the Snowy and Howitt plains are pretty flat, with not many trees because they are above the snowline. If it's cool, there may be snow too. I've got an article from the walking club's newsletter on the place, Phryne. It might be helpful. Who's your copilot?'

'Haven't got one,' said Phryne. 'Too dangerous.'

She scanned the newsletter, squinting at the tiny print. *Melbourne Walking Club*, it said. *Buller-Howitt country.*

'Thanks, Bunji. Can you get onto Shell and tell them to get a full load of fuel to Talbotville and Mansfield for me? I'll start in two days, to allow them to get there first.'

'Can't you wait until Saturday? Then I can come too.'

'No. I said I'm in a hurry, and it's far too dangerous to take a friend. And I might have a passenger on the return trip. Ask

Bill McNaughton to go over the Moth for me, will you? New spark plugs, check the tyres, that sort of thing.'

'No, not Bill,' said Bunji in a determined manner. 'I'll go over your Moth. Now remember what I've said about mountains. Fly above cloud if you can, below it if you must, but never fly in cloud. It will kill you, nine times out of ten. Keep awake. Mountains are not forgiving. There's not going to be a nice flat paddock to glide down to if you run into trouble. Keep as low as you can. You'll know if you're icing because the wings get heavy and unresponsive.'

'And if the wings are iced?'

'Land somewhere. If in trees, aim to shear the tops, that'll slow your rate of descent.'

'And tear the wings off?'

'Yes, of course, but you might get out alive.'

'Hmmm,' said Phryne. She finished her tea and stood up, rolling the maps.

'I'll study these. I'd better send a message to Talbotville too, and tell them to expect me. I don't suppose they have many planes drop in on them. Thanks, Bunji,' she added, and went out to watch the student fliers taking their first tentative steps toward being airborne.

Bunji Ross sighed. She considered Phryne to lack the caution that made for long-lived fliers.

Phryne sent a telegram to 'Postmaster, Talbotville' warning him that she was about to descend on his town and asking that a windsock be put up next to a suitable landing place. Phryne's Gipsy Moth, called Rigel, was capable of landing on a continuous strip less than one hundred yards long, and had a stalling speed of 40 mph. She was waylaid by Bill McNaughton, full of news about the new Leopard Moth.

'It has brakes, Miss Fisher, you must admit that this is a huge improvement on the basic design.'

'Yes, but wouldn't it be hard on the tyres? Surely braking will gouge great lumps out of them. They're only rubber, you know.'

'True, but there is a new tyre design as well. She's a pretty machine, Miss Fisher. You know that I gave my heart to the Fokker, but the Leopard Moth is pretty good.'

'Well, Bill, I'll think about it. I may need a new plane if my next trip is as hairy as Bunji seems to think.'

Bill McNaughton stooped down from his six-foot height, massive brow corrugated with thought.

'Bunji thinks it's dangerous? Then it must be. Sporting flier, that girl. Where are you going?'

'Over the Australian Alps,' said Phryne, unrolling her map to demonstrate the route. 'North-east to Mansfield, then across Buller and into this valley, the Wonnangatta Valley, then to a place called Talbotville.'

'They look like pretty high mountains,' he commented, taking the map. 'Is this the latest map? Looks a hundred years old.'

'Mountains generally stay where they are put.'

'Hmm. Well, I'll put in the order for the Leopard. You never know, you might get out of the crash alive. But I'll be sorry to see her go, the little Moth. Nice little bus. Got to go, I've three new fliers panting for the air. Good luck, Phryne.' Bill McNaughton strode off, and Phryne took herself soberly home.

'You're going alone!' Dot dropped one of the shoes she was holding.

'Yes, of course. I don't want anyone else getting ki—I mean, I like flying alone.'

'It's dangerous, isn't it?' Dot demanded. 'Take me!'

'Don't be silly, Dot, you've never been in the air before.'

'I can learn.' Dot's mouth firmed into a determined line. 'It can't be that difficult. Lots of ladies can fly.'

'No, Dot.'

'But...' began Dot, and Phryne sat her down on the couch, taking the other shoe gently out of her hand.

'No, Dot. I am not taking anyone. You shall stay here and go to the Policemen and Firemen's Ball in that beautiful dress with your charming policeman Hugh, and you will have a lovely time. I will be fine. I am a good flier and I have maps and a compass and I will find my way home, you see if I don't. I have been altogether too safe and comfortable for too long and I need a bit of danger. I have been suffocating in this over-civilized atmosphere of jazz and drink and I have to get out of it for a bit. You can see that, can't you?'

Dot couldn't. Her idea of perfection, after a very hard-working childhood and a traumatic life as a servant before Phryne had rescued her, was one long band of monotony in which nothing out-of-the-way occurred. Phryne divined this, and sighed.

'We will never really understand each other, Dot dear,' she said sadly. 'But at least we can accept each other. I need adventure, you need quiet; well, you shall stay and be calm, and I shall go off and be adventurous. You wouldn't like flying, Dot darling, you really wouldn't. And I would be worrying about you instead of myself and the plane, and that would not be helpful. Or safe. Now, that's settled. Dig out all my flying gear, will you, and see that nothing needs mending or replacing. See, here are the maps.'

She traced out her route, Dot leaning over her shoulder, and talked learnedly of fuel dumps and weight-to-lift ratios, and Dot listened politely without having the faintest idea what Phryne was talking about. As requested, she went to the wardrobe and pulled out the flying gear. Helmet, scarf, long winter woollies, trousers and shirt, and sheepskin-lined boots and coat. She was not, however, happy. Her mad mistress was off on some tearing folly of her own again, and Dot would not stop worrying until Phryne was safely back in her own house, dressing for dinner and behaving like a lady should.

Phryne then rang Hilliers and ordered the largest box of best-quality chocolates that they made.

Mr. Butler answered the phone as Phryne was consulting with Dot over a strange rubber funnel and tube Dot had found in the case, which Phryne took when flying.

'What is it, Miss?'

'Dot dear, I don't quite know how to reply without offending your modesty. Think of the shape of that soft funnelly thing, and of the number of hours one has to spend in the air, and the consequent strain on the human bladder. Yes, Mr. Butler?'

Mr. Butler had arrived in the nick of time, as Phryne's explanation was becoming too explicit. Dot nodded and blushed.

'Shell Oil, Miss, to convey the message that fuel will be waiting at Mansfield and at Talbotville on Friday.'

'Super.'

'Also, Hilliers have delivered a large box of chocolates.'

'Good.'

Mr. Butler cast a curious glance at the rubber tube, which Dot had thrust under a cushion, and took his leave.

'Well, Dot?'

'A very useful idea, Miss. Handy to take on a picnic, as the little girl said when she saw her brother peeing against a tree. There is a hole in your trousers, Miss, looks like a cigarette burn. Shall I mend it?'

'Yes please, Dot.'

'All the rest of the gear is in good condition, though the boots are wearing through on the outside edges. I reckon they'll make one more flight. What do you want to pack, Miss?'

Dot was bearing up bravely under her fears for Phryne, and the least Phryne could do was cooperate.

'Very little, Dot, weight is always a consideration in the air. Some undies and another shirt. That will do, I think. Cigarettes, of course, money, the little gun…'

'You are expecting trouble?'

'Only from passing snakes, Dot, don't fret.' Phryne did not mention that it was not unusual for pilots to carry a gun. It was generally thought that if one was crashing in a burning plane, one might have time for a suitable suicide. Phryne, in her earthbound moments, considered it unlikely that in such a situation one would have the presence of mind to find, load, and fire a pistol, but airborne, the presence of the gun was comforting.

'When are you leaving, Miss?'

'Friday. I have to allow time for the oil company to convey my fuel. And it depends on the weather. Apparently there is a weather station of sorts on Buller; I shall be able to consult it when I get to Mansfield. I may be away for three days, Dot, or it may be a week or more, if the weather turns nasty in the mountains. You will go to that ball, Dot, and wear the sunrise dress?'

'Yes, Miss.' Dot's voice sounded flat.

'You promise?'

'Yes, Miss, I promise.' Dot added, 'If you will be careful.'

'I'll be careful.'

'Promise?' Dot turned to glare at Phryne. Phryne sighed.

'Promise.'

◇◇◇

She was studying the maps and *Regulations of the Operation of Aircraft* (1920) after dinner that night when Iris Jordan was announced.

Iris swept in, radiating health as usual, pushing a frail girl before her.

'I thought you might like to see how Miss King was getting on,' she announced. Phryne jumped to her feet.

'Miss King! You are walking again!'

Miss King blushed, smiled, and demonstrated, walking to the end of the parlour and back with only a slight stiffness to betray the fact that she had almost danced herself into paralysis.

'Very good, very good indeed! Miss Jordan, you are amazing.'

'It was nothing. A matter of working with the body, not against it. If she had not been wearing a Louis heel we should have been all better yesterday. However, a little more work and Miss King's cooperation and we shall have her dancing at her own wedding.'

Clearly the relationship between masseuse and massaged had become close.

'Do sit down, ladies, and have some tea, or perhaps a drink?'

'I can't, Miss Fisher, thanks ever so, but Percy is waiting outside,' said Miss King, blushing again. 'We've got...'

'…the car?' finished Phryne. 'Let's go and have a look, then.'

She escorted Violet King down the steps, which she took like a two-year-old, and surveyed the bright white Austin. Percy McPhee was standing next to it, smoking a gasper which he threw away as soon as he saw Miss Fisher approaching.

'Well, Mr. McPhee, what a nice little car, and so new!'

'Er, thanks, Miss Fisher, they delivered it today. You must have really put the frighteners on them, they registered it and all. I was saving up for the registration, now we've got some extra lolly. And Miss Jordan has been kind enough to unkink my legs, too, so we're off to get married on Saturday and we'd like you to come to the wedding.'

'Sorry, Mr. McPhee, I'm flying off on Friday and I don't know when I'll be back. Thanks for the invitation. Is the exchange all made, then?'

'I drove up yesterday and arranged it all. Bloke wants to start right off. He's got a horse and cart so we'll swap at my dad's place, he can go to Queensland and we'll have transport to the farm. Bonzer place. He just put in a hundred new pear trees. Cows are all in milk.'

Percy McPhee's eyes were bright for a man who must have driven half a day to get to the farm and half a day back. Violet leaned on his shoulder with an expression of lamb-like trust which Phryne found very touching.

'Well, good luck, then, and have a good journey,' she said, stepping back. Percy McPhee grabbed her hand and Violet kissed her.

'We couldn't never have done it without you,' said Violet.

'No, my dears, you did it yourselves, by dancing yourselves to a nub.'

'I wish we could do something for you,' said Violet wistfully.

'Oh, you can, you can,' said Phryne quickly, aware of the burden which gratitude could be. 'Do you have white peaches?' Percy McPhee nodded. 'They are my favourite fruit, I can never get enough of them, and most of the fruiterers prefer cling peaches. Send me a case of white peaches when they are next ripe. I have always wanted to have enough white peaches to bathe in. Goodbye,' she added. Percy started the engine carefully and pulled away from the pavement.

Iris Jordan and Phryne watched the terribly new, bright little car drive away.

'Well, that's one happy ending,' said Phryne. 'Pity the others don't work out so neatly. Come in, Miss Jordan, unless you are in a hurry?'

'No, I'm not in a hurry. I just wanted to show you how Miss King had recovered. And to talk about...'

'Yes, quite. But not on the street.'

Phryne seated her guest in the softest armchair and provided her with freshly squeezed orange juice, at her request. Iris coughed, took a sip of juice, started to speak, took another sip and finally said, 'You know who did that murder, don't you?'

Phryne nodded.

'How can you just leave it like that?' cried Iris, her ruddy complexion paling.

'Why not? I'm not the Masked Avenger of the penny novel. I have no particular interest in Truth or Justice. I haven't even got a good definition of Truth or Justice. There are always redeeming features. Bernard Stevens, the victim, was an unpleasant little person with a talent for blackmail. Because of Stevens' death, I managed to avert a scandal which would have destroyed an innocent party; well, relatively innocent. Because Stevens died, McPhee and King won the dance competition and, possibly, their chance at happiness. On the other hand, presumably someone loved and will miss Stevens.'

'But, you leave it.'

'For the moment. As I see it, it is someone else's problem.'

'I should have stuck to massage.' Iris rubbed her forehead. 'Massage is simple. Just a matter of knowing how the muscles and nerves work, and encouraging them to heal. People are so complicated!'

'Now, I'm going off flying on Friday. When I get back I will Tell All.'

Iris set down her glass and rose effortlessly to her feet from the depths of the chair.

'It's a mess, isn't it?' she asked sadly.

'Yes.' Phryne patted her muscular shoulder. 'It is a mess, all right.'

Chapter Ten

When constabulary duty's to be done, to be done,
A policeman's lot is not a happy one.

Pirates of Penzance, Gilbert and Sullivan

Thursday dawned bright and clear. Phryne sniffed the air delightedly as she took a morning walk along the seashore. No one on the beach but herself and a selection of the cleanest seagulls she had ever seen. They followed her in swooping, squabbling curves, snatching up the bread she threw. She watched them with quiet pleasure. Ah, to fly like a gull, to feel the wind under her own flesh-and-feather wings, the lift, the swoop, the pressure of the air! A group of pelicans spiralled into an updraft, looping and gliding with unstudied grace.

Phryne threw the remains of the bread to the gulls and reflected that it had been too long since she had flown. Even the presence of a noisy engine and the stench of oil and aeroplane dope and canvas could not detract from the intoxicating pleasure of flying above the world when all others were forced to crawl like ants on the surface.

Dot was packing the small case, hoping not to find anything more which might challenge her modesty.

'What's this? Darning needles and string?'

'Yes, to sew on a patch. That tin is aircraft dope, don't open it.'

'But, Miss, you can't sew!' Phryne's inability to embroider was legendary.

'All you need to repair a plane is herringbone stitch, Dot, and I learned that from Irish Michael at the RFC base in England. It was near my school. I didn't learn to embroider because I couldn't see any point in it, but it's different when there is a reason. If you want any herringbone stitched, I'm your woman.'

Dot folded a piece of canvas carefully and packed it around the miscellaneous contents. Spark plugs, a spanner, some spare undies, some compounded chocolate and raisins, a flask of brandy, needle and thread, aircraft dope, a powder compact, two screwdrivers and a nail file, a spare pair of socks and a silk stocking.

'Why the stocking?'

'Filter for aviation fuel,' said Phryne. 'Well, that's everything. I'm going to study my maps again, Dot.'

North and east to Mansfield, Phryne considered, should not present too many problems. Up and over Kinglake and bearing east for Lake Eildon, which looked to be a sizeable bit of water, and Mansfield at the end of the top spur of the lake. It was after Mansfield that the flying would become dangerous. Some of the alps were over six thousand feet high. Air began to get thin up there, and it would be punishingly cold. Lumpy country, Bunji had said; lumpy meant lethal. Bunji had flown over the Himalayas, the roof of the world, and lived, but Phryne knew that Bunji was a much more skilled flier than she would ever be.

Nevertheless, Phryne was not in the mood to trek on packhorse at ten miles an hour across all that mountainous wilderness. People lived there. They must know the ways in and out. And all she needed for success was a cool head and a clear day. Over Buller would be best, she thought, counting the peaks; then fly between Speculation and Mount Howitt and follow the river valley of the Wonnangatta, turn sharp east across Mount Cynthia and Crooked

River and down to Talbotville. She found the newsletter which Bunji had given her and settled down to read.

'Hmm,' she said aloud after five minutes. 'Gold, eh? I thought all the gold rushes were to Bendigo and Ballarat and central Victoria. It just shows how much they didn't tell me at school. I always suspected it.' She read on. Gold had been found in Crooked River and Black Snake Creek; alluvial gold, close to the surface. There had been a rush and several towns were established: Grant, Howittville, Crooked River, Hogtown, Winchester, Mayfair. All of them had been deserted when the gold ran out, except Grant, which closed down in 1923 when the post office (Prop. Albert Stout) moved to Talbotville, the only gold town still in operation in the area. She saw that Talbotville was on the Crooked River, next east from Wonnangatta.

'And, by the look of it, it's the only town at all before Dargo,' commented Phryne. 'I wish this print were clearer! Talbotville seems to be the depot for all of this huge mountainous area! How isolated they must be, the settlers out there in—what did young Victor call it? The great silence. What lovely names they had for the reefs! Rose of Australia, Great Western, Morning Star, Good Hope, Pioneer, St. Leger, Moonlight!'

Phryne dined alone and went to sleep, wondering about a gold reef called Moonlight.

Friday morning was cool and when Phryne arose and looked over the sea there was not a cloud in the sky.

The phone rang while she was breakfasting on kedgeree, toast, fried eggs and muffins. The prospect of danger always made her hungry.

'Detective Inspector Robinson, Miss Fisher.'

Phryne took a quick gulp of coffee and went to the receiver.

'Good morning, Jack!' she said brightly.

'Rang you to say that we are releasing your friend Charles Freeman.' The policman's voice was cold. 'Thanks and all for finding him, but he couldn't have done it. Two witnesses place him too far from the body.'

'Oh, well, sorry about that, Jack dear.'

'You know more about this than meets the eye, Miss Fisher. Now look, I been a good friend to you. I handed over them dirty pictures to get your nancy-boy off the hook, when I could have given 'em to Vice, and I should have, too. If you know who did this you could at least be a mate and tell me.'

'Not now, Jack. I'm flying off to Gippsland today.'

'Flying? What, over the Alps? Isn't that very dangerous?'

'Yes, very. I might crash. And if so I will not be interfering in any of your cases again.'

'Don't say that.' He sounded abashed. 'I don't want to lose you, Miss Fisher, I'm just asking for your cooperation.'

'I tell you what, Jack dear, I think I do know who did it, and how, and when I get back I shall tell you all about it.'

'Promise?'

'On my word.'

Jack Robinson had a high opinion of the honour of women, especially Phryne's. He had never known her to break her word.

'Very well, Miss Fisher. I'll see you when you get back.'

'Well, Jack, good luck with the case. Oh, by the way, I meant to ask—what about Miss Shore, the dead man's partner? How is she?'

'She's been released, Miss, from hospital. She didn't see nothing useful. Such a to-do I never saw!' Jack Robinson chuckled. 'Her mother and three sisters and relatives all over the place all refusing to let me speak to "poor little Pansy" until she was quite better, and poor little Pansy collapsing back against her pillow and promising to go home and be a good girl in future. She wasn't close to the dead man, Miss Fisher. She answered an advertisement in the paper for a partner. Says he promised her ten quid and half the prize if they won.'

'Put me down for the ten quid,' said Phryne.

'No need, Miss, a friend of Bernard Stevens has paid it, the one who wasn't in any of them photos what never went through the evidence register and you didn't return to him. He made it twenty quid and pleased to do it, by the look of him. And paid her hospital bill. Nice young gentleman, you'd never think he was...'

'What he is. Good. I like my loose ends all tied up. Well, if I don't see you again, Jack, it's been nice working with you.'

'Don't say that, Miss Fisher. You'll be back.'

'Is that one of those Sherlock Holmes intuitions?'

'Yes,' said Detective Inspector Robinson firmly. 'It is. Happy flying,' he added, and rang off.

Mrs. Butler came out to the car with a wicker picnic hamper and a thermos flask.

'Black coffee as you asked, Miss, and the sandwiches and so on. I've put in that big box of chocolates and some biscuits.'

'Thank you, Mrs. Butler, I'm sure they'll be lovely.' Mrs. Butler stepped off the running board and surveyed Phryne in her flying gear with an indulgent eye.

'You have a nice fly, Miss, and come back safe,' she said. 'Off you go, Mr. B.'

◇◇◇

Two men manoeuvred the Moth Rigel out of the hangar and onto the smooth tarmac.

'Well, old girl,' said Bunji Ross, 'I've taken down your engine and rebuilt it. There was a split pin which some idiot replaced with a bit of wire that was just about to shear. You have new spark plugs and she's tuned to a hair. Now, you will remember about not flying in cloud, won't you? Get above or below it. Got the maps? Good.'

Bunji boosted Phryne into the cockpit of the two-seater Gipsy Moth. Its blue and yellow paint gleamed in the pale sunlight. Phryne packed her case and assorted goodies into the empty copilot's seat and went into her preflight checks. 'Never take a machine into the air unless you are confident that it will fly,' warned the *Regulations for Operation of Aircraft*, and Phryne checked that her flaps flapped and her compass was working.

'Switch off,' she yelled above the sudden roar. 'Goodbye, Dot! Be good, and don't worry! Suck in! Give my best regards to Hugh, won't you? One, two, three, go!' she shrieked. Bunji spun the propeller, the engine caught and turned over, and the Moth called after a star trundled forward, got up speed, and leapt up into the air.

Dot watched as Phryne took the little plane into a wide circle, her leather-helmeted and goggled head still visible. She wondered if that would be the last anyone saw of Phryne. Mr. Butler put a hand on her shoulder.

'Come along, Dot, let's go home. She'll be all right. Terribly lucky, she is. After all, she's got us, eh? Come on, now. Home we go and a nice cuppa,' said Mr. Butler, who was convinced that tea was the cure for most female ills, from miscarriage to bankruptcy. Dot tore her gaze away from the sky and climbed into the big car. There was now nothing at all she could do to help Phryne except to obey her last command, which was not to worry. Absurd. How could she not worry?

Mr. Butler, at least, drove like a sensible citizen, and gave Dot no further shocks on the way home.

Chapter Eleven

Up in the air, sky high,
sky high

Patience, Gilbert and Sullivan

The tricky part about flying, Phryne thought as the wind tore past
her goggles and the earth released the plane, was taking off and
landing. Once in the air, a Gipsy Moth would continue until it
ran out of fuel or met very adverse conditions. A Moth did not
lumber into the air, dragging itself up in defiance of gravity, but
side-slipped the clutch of the earth and leapt into the embrace
of the air like a dog jumping up onto a loved master's chest. A
Moth fooled the force that pulled everything down, rather than
defied it. She climbed to five thousand feet and turned the plane
north and a little east, taking her sightings from the ground.

It was a perfect day for flying, such cloud as there was
plumped high, white, and right out of reach. The ground was
clearer than print. Little cars crawled like beetles across the slow
earth; small roads like ribbons snaked below.

'I'm out of all of that,' Phryne sang to herself, 'far above all
that striving and all those people; high up in the sky, and nothing
else aloft, either; what could be better?'

She flew directly north-east over the patch of forest and water that was Kinglake before she reached for her thermos and let go the controls. Rigel flew straight and level while she poured her coffee and drank it in a mood of quiet exultation.

Phryne took the craft up to seven thousand feet, where the ground came closer; she was flying over mountains.

'That must be Mount Despair. If it is Mount Mitchell, I'm off course. I shall know soon; I should cross the River Acheron about now—and there it is. I wonder who named these places? They must have been lost. Poor things. This is a terribly big country, isn't it?' Phryne usually talked to herself in the air. 'Aha. That huge big stretch of water must be Lake Eildon, and Mansfield is at the furthest bit. I hope there is somewhere to land there. Shell should have warned the locals. I wonder if they've seen a plane before? Goodness. The surrounding hills are rather steep, aren't they? Up a bit, Rigel, my dear.'

She flew higher over Lake Eildon, and people in boats waved as she passed.

'Just the one lump and that should be Mansfield. Good. I think I'll try following the road.'

She flew along the looping string which was the road, and was surprised by an abrupt mountain, the road cutting deeply through it. She flicked the little plane up into the sky again, passed the mountain, dropped again to the peaceful township of Mansfield, and circled until she sighted a drooping windsock and a long path cleared in a paddock.

'Down we go,' she told herself firmly. 'Landing is just the same as taking off, in reverse, that's what Bunji says.' There was no discernable wind and she made her approach from the east. There were a lot of people on the ground, including every child within a hundred miles, and Phryne hoped that she was not about to make an idiot of herself in front of the entire population of central Victoria. Rigel dipped, losing speed. Phryne estimated that she must be getting low on fuel. At least, if she crashed, there was less chance of fire. She came in like a duck landing, swooping and wobbling, until the wheels touched the very beginning of the cleared path and the machine ran smoothly to a textbook halt.

It was a lot better than most of Phryne's landings. One of her instructors had told her that any landing was good which did not break the plane, and Phryne's landings definitely came into that category.

Part of her problem, she considered, was that she didn't want to land. Flying was as close as she came to pure pleasure in which no one but herself need be considered.

She switched off the engine, and the propeller spun to a halt. Phryne jumped down, a little stiff, and decided that the still air posed no threat and that she did not need to tie Rigel down with her tent-pegs and ropes. A gust of ground wind could turn the plane over and break her frame; but here it was still and hot.

Phryne pulled off her helmet to catch the first child who belted past her to get into the plane.

'Hold it!' she said sternly. 'You can look, but don't touch. One kick of those boots could go right through my wings!' The child turned in her grasp, hearing her voice.

'Mum!' he screamed. 'Mum! It's a lady!'

Phryne put him down. The crowd was approaching.

'My God,' said a fat storekeeper, wiping his hands on his white apron, 'the nipper's right. It is a woman.'

'What do you mean, "it"?' asked Phryne. 'Is this a nice welcome from the city of Mansfield?'

'Beg pardon, Miss, we wasn't expecting a lady, that's all,' said a tall, slow-speaking young man. 'Your fuel's arrived, Miss. Shall we bring it over? If you'd like a cuppa, the Missus has it all ready.'

'Nice to meet you,' said Phryne with feeling. She had not been looking forward to carrying all those fuel cans. 'Thanks, I'd love some tea. Phryne Fisher.' She offered her hand. He took it and shook it heartily.

'Tim Wallace. Glad to meet yer. This is Miss Fisher, Mum,' he added to a stout woman, who smiled and pushed back her straying grey hair.

'Nice to see you, Miss. This way.' She conducted Phryne off the path into the shade of trees. A fire had been lit and a billy was boiling. The rest of the crowd divided equally between Phryne and the plane as chief attractions.

'Mr. Wallace, can you keep the kids off the bus? They are welcome to look, but she's fragile,' said Phryne, and the tall man grinned, grabbing a running child under one arm.

'She'll be apples,' he promised, and Phryne left it in his capable hands.

Mrs. Wallace did not ask how Phryne took her tea, but pushed into her hand a large tin mug, already loaded with sugar and milk. Phryne bent and stretched, getting the kinks out of her spine, watched by a silent mob.

'What's it like, up there in the sky?' a child asked. Phryne gulped some tea and smiled.

'It's lovely,' she said. 'Lovely and high and far away.'

'Is she fast?' asked the boy.

'Cruising speed of eighty miles an hour. What's the weather been like here?'

'Clear and hot,' said a farmer. 'We need rain.'

'What about the mountains?'

'Clear as well. Buller sent to say that cloud is at ten thousand feet,' said a man who was evidently the postmaster. 'Should stay clear, but the Snowies are funny. Can blizzard without any warning. You want to be careful, Miss.'

'I shall.' She smiled. Mrs. Wallace patted her, unexpectedly.

'I think it's wonderful,' she said combatively, as though defying public opinion. 'The things girls can do today. And them things, them planes, they could do a lot for us. Get supplies in when snow cuts the roads. Get sick people out. I think you're very brave, Miss, and good luck to yer.'

The watching men muttered, but no one seemed willing to take Mrs. Wallace on in argument. Phryne smiled.

'When I come back I'll have time to give someone a ride,' she said mischievously. 'Who shall it be?'

There was an uneasy shuffle, as of people walking backwards. Tim Wallace, who had supervised the loading of the fuel, came to tell Phryne her plane was free of children and full of petrol, and called, 'Me!' to his compatriots' evident relief.

'Yair, Tim'll go up with yer,' said Mrs. Wallace proudly.

'Thanks for the tea, and I'll be back soon,' said Phryne, shaking Mrs. Wallace's hand and walking back to Rigel. 'Now, can I have one helper and everyone else get right back. Away you go, kids, this prop is not for decoration, you know. All right.'

She climbed up into the cockpit and pulled on her helmet. 'You stand this side of the prop, Mr. Wallace, and when I say go, you pull it down toward you and get your hands out of the way very smartly. All right? Switch on.' She did so, and listened to the revs build up, looking ahead at the fence at the end of her runway and hoping that she would be airborne before she met it. 'Suck in, one, two, three—go!' Tim Wallace swung the prop, retaining his hands, to Phryne's relief, and the Moth bounced forward, wobbled a little over a few stones, then jumped up into the sky.

Phryne soared up to circle at a safe height, waved, consulted her compass, and flew east and a little south, straight for the mountains which loomed high, dark, and still crowned with snow, directly in her path.

Chapter Twelve

*If I'm feeling tomorrow like I feel today
I'm gonna pack my trunk and I'm gonna make
my getaway*

'St. Louis Blues,' W. C. Handy

Phryne had memorized her maps, such as they were, and thus felt that strange, disorienting click when the landscape below swam into resemblance. It was like the sense of correctness when she found the right radio wavelength after swinging across the broadcast. There, below the little plane, was the valley she was seeking. She flew in over the peculiar rocky crown of the Viking and headed down the Wonnangatta Valley from its secret beginning in the Terrible Hollow. Turning sharp east, she surmounted Mount Cynthia and dropped down into the defile of Crooked River.

No place to land here. Rocks, a wilderness of trees. If anything happened, the chances of her surviving were remote. Then the valley widened out. She flew over a homestead, sitting neatly like a toy house in a rich wet plain, and down thirty miles to where she fervently hoped Talbotville was waiting for her. The air was still clear, but clouds appeared to be coming down. It was very cold and there was snow on the Snowy Plains and on the Howitt Plains. Snow in October! Phryne drank the last of her coffee and flexed her fingers in their sheepskin-lined gauntlets, trying to get some feeling back into them.

There, below, was a cleared strip along the edge of the water, and a windsock streaming north. Good. It stood to reason that the only wind which could get into this valley would blow either south or north. Into the wind she circled, observing that the windsock was a real sock. There was activity on the ground.

Down, down, Phryne piloted Rigel, until she was skimming along at treetop height. The strip was not very long. She allowed the Moth to drop until her wheels touched, cut the engine, and wished she had waited for the Leopard Moth with brakes. Rigel belted along the strip at forty miles an hour, and Phryne turned her as she neared the fence so that she would at least preserve the propeller if she had to hit something. People were shouting. Luckily, the strip was mostly mud. Rigel lost speed rapidly, and finally rolled to a stop ten yards from the fence.

'Thank goodness for a solid river-valley quagmire,' breathed Phryne, and stepped out of the plane into a churned-up sog of rich, black mud.

Filled with the strong sense of relief which always accompanied one of her landings, Phryne slogged forward and was extracted from an unusually deep hole by a strong, thin, tanned woman in riding breeches.

'Welcome to Talbotville,' she said, and beamed. Phryne was pleased. This was better than Mansfield's 'My God, it's a woman.' The 'it' rankled. She smiled into the tall woman's face.

'Thank you! Nice strip you've dug. And thanks for the windsock. I'm Phryne Fisher.'

'Anne Purvis. This is Jo.'

Another charming smile from a smaller but plumper woman in a divided skirt and a man's tweed jacket. She had amiable brown eyes which were nevertheless not eyes one would wish to try to take advantage of, and curly brown hair. 'Josephine Binet.'

'The writer?' asked Phryne, interested. 'I've read your *Murder by the Stockyard Fence*. It was excellent. I usually guess who did it in the first three chapters and I didn't work yours out until chapter ten.'

'I'll let you into a secret,' confided Jo Binet, leading Phryne over a small creek and up onto a track. 'That's when I guessed, too. Come into town. Not much of a town, I admit, but a town nonetheless.'

Three wiry young men hovered around the plane. Phryne looked back severely.

'You can look all you like but don't put one of those boots near my wing, gentlemen. It's fragile. If the fuel's come I'll take you up for a spin—if I can ever take off again. Maybe tomorrow. Is there any crosswind in this valley?'

Heads in battered felt hats inclined towards one another, as if taking counsel. The middle head shook.

'Nah, no crosswind, Missus.'

'Good, then I won't need to tie her down. Now, ladies, a cup of tea would be greeted with some relief. It's very cold up there.'

'The postmaster says there'll be snow. He always knows about weather, does Albert Stout. Just up along here, Miss Fisher, and you shall have tea.'

'Tell me, Miss Binet, why do you live here? I mean, writers usually live in the city, near to publishers and agents and cafés. I always understood that a café was essential for the creative process.'

Josephine Binet stopped in what, for want of another term, would be called the main street of Talbotville, and said simply, 'Look.'

Phryne looked. Although she was cold and a little shaken, and longed desperately for tea, she could not fail to be impressed by the landscape. High and blue, cold and distant, the mountains sat comfortably in their warm fluff of forest. Snow gums of amazing height soared above her, coloured like a Paris fashion show and with bark of silk. The massive river valley, slab-sided with granite, was capped by an improbably blue sky and looked as if Gothic cathedrals had plummeted, spires down, into rich wet earth. At her feet, small pink orchids grew under the fronded black wattle. The air smelt of woodsmoke and growing things, with a faint, pure hint of snow.

'Yes,' agreed Phryne. 'I see.'

'Tea and scones,' said Anne Purvis, pulling at Phryne's other hand. 'Landscape will wait.'

Talbotville nestled into the lumpy surroundings as though it had grown there. It had twelve houses constructed of wood and roofed with iron, and several huts of the old fashion, roofed with wooden shingles and walled with round saplings.

'We've got one of the houses, because Jo can't stand spiders,' said Anne, leading the way through a small crowd of people who were staring at Phryne as though she had dropped in from Mars. A child stuck his thumb in his mouth and backed away when she smiled at him. Another ran screaming for her mother.

'They aren't used to the helmet,' explained Anne, and Phryne removed the offending headgear. The child uncorked his thumb and returned the smile.

'I like the old bark huts, but they are terrible spider traps,' explained Anne. 'Do come in.'

The house was of three rooms, one of which was given over to a typewriter, a pile of paper, and hundreds of books—some stacked on raw wood shelves, but most lying on the floor, piled, or open, or marked with slips of blue paper. The middle room had a large colonial stove filling one fireplace and a sparkling rosy 'company' fire in the other. Neatly piled in one corner was a doctor's bag, a saddle, some horse accoutrements in various stages of repair, and a folded, starched white apron.

Anne heaved the kettle onto the top of the stove and motioned Phryne to an easy chair.

'If we've got nothing to do, we mend harnesses,' complained Jo. 'Luckily I have ten thumbs. Would you like to take off your boots?'

'Not yet, my feet are still frozen. Why harnesses?'

Anne was up to her elbows in flour. It was a bush cook's boast that she could have the scones ready by the time the kettle boiled, and she was not going to be outdone.

'Anne's the local nurse,' explained Josephine. 'She always gets called out in the worst weather, and the only way to get to some of these places is on a horse. We keep the horse in the publican's stable, but Anne's fussy about her saddle.'

'Quite right,' agreed Phryne. 'A badly kept saddle can gall the horse, and it doesn't do the rider any good either.'

Neither of these women, although they must be bursting with curiosity, had asked her what she was doing in Talbotville. Phryne had thought that delicacy had gone out of fashion. She was pleased to find it alive and well in Gippsland. Anne punched down her scone dough with the solid soggy noise that promised good results. Mrs. Butler had informed Phryne that to make good scones one had to be strong, and Anne certainly looked strong, with a horseman's strength of sinew and bone. Josephine looked more used to civilization. Phryne decided to ask.

'Were you born out here, Anne?'

'Was mustering other side of Kosciusko before I could walk,' the young woman grinned. 'But Dad wouldn't let me run me own cattle, so I went to school and learned to be a nurse. And,' she added, cutting out the scones with a passionfruit pulp tin, 'I've ridden wilder rides as a nurse than I ever did wheeling bulls in the scrub. My oath! Remember Mrs. Johnson's baby, Jo?'

'What happened to Mrs. Johnson's baby?' asked Phryne, feeling her toes begin to thaw.

'She had it in the middle of the night,' said Josephine in her golden-syrup voice. 'Silly chook should have known it was coming, it was her fifth, but her boy comes galloping up at piccaninny daylight to fetch Anne. "Mum is bad," he said, so Anne goes off with him, and comes back straight down the mountain, scattering flints like the Man from Snowy River with this white bundle on the saddle-bow. My heart was in my mouth. It was Mrs. Johnson's latest, wrapped up in her apron—distressed, Anne said. After that ride it should have been scared out of its wits. But babies are tough.'

'Did it survive?'

'You met it in the street.' said Anne, 'Kid with the thumb in his mouth. I've ordered some bitter aloes from Bairnsdale for him. Jeez, I was cold, but Jo went crook about me cold feet. Anyway, why shouldn't I ride like the Man from Snowy River? I was brought up near there. My dad knew him. Jack Riley. Nice bloke, Dad said.' She slotted the trays of scones into the oven and closed the door with a clap, stirred the fire inside with a short poker, and rubbed flour off her hands.

'Scones'll be on in ten minutes,' she said with quiet pride.

With the comment about the cold feet Phryne realized that there was only one bedroom in the house and only one bed, and that two women lived there. She blinked. She realized that Josephine and Anne were watching her with polite patience, waiting for it to dawn upon her. Phryne smiled.

'What do the locals think?' she asked.

Josephine answered with a laugh. 'They don't think anything. Nothing wrong with two women living together. It's not even illegal. Now, is there anything you want to ask us in private, before we let the chaps in? They'll be champing at the bit about the plane out there, and their tongues'll be hanging out for Anne's tea and scones.'

'Yes. I have come to look for a man who has been missing for years. He ran away from the Great War and never went back.'

Silence fell. The kettle began to sing. Two intelligent faces, quite unalike except for the expression, stared at her.

'What was this man's name?' asked Anne huskily.

'Freeman,' said Phryne, holding their gaze. 'Victor Ernest Freeman. His father is dead. I don't think he knows that. There is a question of inheritance. I tried phoning here, but the postmaster hung up on me.'

'If he's been missing all this while, then perhaps he doesn't want to be found,' said Josephine coolly. 'Why disturb him?'

'I don't want to disturb him. I just want to know if he's alive. His brother also wants to find him. He thought he was dead.'

'Perhaps he is by now.'

'Or perhaps not. He was living up at MacAlister Springs,' said Phryne. 'He wrote to his father from there. Now, can you tell me if he's still there? I will leave him alone if he doesn't want to have anything to do with the world, and might I say in parenthesis that his family is utterly ghastly and I wouldn't blame him for a moment if he never wants to see any of them again. I'll leave him be if he wants to be alone with the mountains.'

'How did you know he wanted to be alone…' began Josephine.

'With the mountains? I read his letters to his father. The great silence, he called it. Have a heart, ladies, or shall I ask the men?'

'No, don't do that.' Josephine consulted Anne in a glance. 'Don't tell them that's where you are going. They like Vic. We all do. They might try and stop you. Yes, he's still here.' She looked at Anne again, who nodded. 'We'll trust you. Vic Freeman's living in a hut at MacAlister Springs.'

'Jo reckons he's like them old Christian monks—you know, a hermit. A natural religious, she says. But he ain't loopy. Just loves quiet. You'll find him up there all right. And you'll not try and take him back to the city?'

'No, I promise.'

'All right, then. Scones're done. Kettle's boiling. Bring in the blokes, Jo, and mum's the word, eh, Miss Fisher?'

'Phryne, and mum is the word.'

Ten men and several women and four very shy children came into the small house as Anne poured boiling water into the huge teapot and tumbled her scones into several tea cloths. Phryne was supplied with scone, butter and jam, and another huge mug of tea with milk and sugar. It tasted heavenly. The tea was very strong and the scone light, the butter home-made and the jam, in Phryne's honour, shop-bought strawberry.

'Nice place,' said Phryne. 'Beautiful mountains.' She had learned on previous attempts at conversation in the Australian bush to speak slowly and use short sentences. She did not make the mistake of thinking the inhabitants stupid. It was just that they did not talk much and therefore liked to give every word its proper weight. She reflected that a writer might find this touching. Words were seldom given the respect they deserved.

'Yair,' agreed the oldest man present, a gnarled specimen of such legendary toughness that Phryne imagined he shaved with a cross-cut saw. 'She's pretty country all right.' There was a chorus of agreement, muffled in scone.

'Nice machine,' a young man said. 'What sort is it?'

'Gipsy Moth,' said Phryne.

'She fly well?'

'Yes. Eighty miles an hour cruising speed. Will land on a pretty short run, provided it's flat. The valley is ideal.'

'Thinking of getting one,' admitted the young man, to general astonishment. Evidently he had not shared this notion with his fellow Talbotvillians. 'Be bonzer for getting up onto the High Plains.'

'Yes,' agreed Phryne. 'But not many places to land, except here. I came from Mansfield today, and it's very difficult country.'

'Yair,' said the young man. 'But so fast!'

'Also, speed depends on weather and on fuel. Has Shell delivered my fuel, by the way?'

'Yair, fuel cans came in by packhorse from Dargo this morning,' said a stout gentleman in a waistcoat. He was a person of some authority and Phryne guessed he was the postmaster.

'Good. What's the weather report?'

The whole room looked at Albert Stout. He inclined his head, as though listening to the wind.

'Clear for two days,' he opined magisterially. 'Only very high cloud. I doubt even you would fly that high, Miss Fisher!' He paused to chuckle, 'Then, I think, it will close in. There may be more snow, there will certainly be rain.'

'In that case, if some of you would like to come and help me refuel the plane, I had best be off.'

Phryne jammed her warmed feet into her sheepskin boots, reclaimed her jacket from under a sleeping cat and her helmet from an inquisitive child, and stood up.

'You said you'd take me for a ride,' said the young man, identified only as Dave. Phryne took his hand.

'So I shall, but not quite yet. I will return,' she promised, looking with appreciation at the warm room and collaring a scone as she went out. 'Then we shall joyride all around Mount Howitt.'

Refuelled, the Moth was heavier, and Phryne wondered if she had sufficient lift to attain flying speed before she hit the fence.

'Hang on to the wings, friends, and let go when I say "now",' she screamed above the roar of the engine to four straining stockmen. The revs mounted, the Moth shook and rocked. 'Now!' screamed Phryne. They released the wings. Rigel hopped and bounced, approaching the fence at a perilous rate, then leapt into the air.

Phryne gained altitude, breathed a brief prayer of relief, and circled, waving. She mounted the wall of Mount Cynthia, found the Wonnangatta Valley, and flew up over the Snowy Plains.

She turned sharp north, heading for Mount Howitt dead ahead, and was looking out for the small nick in the flat High Plains which marked MacAlister Springs when she flew directly into low cloud and lost all sense of direction, along with her sight.

'Oh, Lord!' she exclaimed ruefully, remembering the *Regulations for Operation of Aircraft*. Do not fly in cloud, it warned sternly. She diverted herself by recalling that it also warned pilot officers not to wear spurs, and wondered what other useless advice it had to offer. Freezing fog flowed past her face. Clouds look so soft from a distance, she thought; up close they were like wet cotton wool. She could not see at all. No light gleamed through to show her where the sun was, and she was rapidly losing remembrance of where it had last been. Her cigarette lighter showed her compass bearing to be due north. She let the little plane drop gradually, hoping to find clear air down lower, not wishing to end her aviation career by being the first woman to fly a Gipsy Moth into Mount Howitt, for which she was still heading at fifty miles an hour. But where was the ground? She lost height, sideslipping a little, her hands numbing on the stick, ice forming on her face.

The wings were getting heavier. The Moth was icing up! Time to land. 'I might even be able to get down in one piece if I could only find where the bloody deck is!' Phryne swore, bit her lip, and strained forward into white murk, colder than the grave. She blinked, noticing that her eyelashes had frozen, and wondered suddenly and horribly if she could have flipped the Moth over in the disorienting cloud, and was even now approaching a nasty and terminal landing, wheels in the air. Is that why she couldn't find the ground?

She fumbled for her lighter and dropped it. To her great relief, it fell down at her feet. She was still the right way up, but that seemed to be the only good thing about the situation.

Appearing with the speed and unreality of ghosts, trees happened in front of her. She throttled the Moth back to stall, and the plane wobbled, complaining. Phryne heard branches crack as the fixed wheels scraped them, saw a clear space in front of her which was evidently placed there by providence, and dropped Rigel neatly into the centre of it. The Moth rolled along grass so flat that it might have been mowed to a perfect landing. Phryne turned off the engine and sat quite still for a full minute. Landed safe, she thought, and I really don't deserve it. I shall have to be a better woman in future.

Brimming with good resolutions, she began to climb out of the Moth, and was doubly astonished to be seized in hard hands and dragged forth, carried over a shoulder, and flung down under a male body ten seconds later.

Chapter Thirteen

BUNTY: *It's such fun, being reminded of things.*
NICKY: *And such agony, too.*

The Vortex, Noel Coward

'Keep down!' hissed a voice in response to her outraged squeak. 'Keep your ears covered. She'll go up in a minute.'

Phryne, relieved that she was not going to have to fight either for her honour or her life, relaxed under the male body and said politely, 'It's unlikely to explode. I wasn't carrying bombs, you know. And that was a very good landing, considering everything. Well, it was a very good landing for me.'

'A woman?' gasped her assailant, and sprang away from her.

Phryne was facing a stocky man, dressed in bush clothing, with long pale hair and a red beard. On top of the Howitt Plains, she reflected, was an odd place to meet the Ancient Mariner.

She stood up carefully and brushed grass off her flying suit. 'I'm a visitor,' she said affably. 'That's my plane, Rigel.'

'The desire of a moth for a star,' quoted the Ancient Mariner in a perfectly normal voice. 'Glad to meet you. Sorry about that. I thought…'

'Yes. Where did you see an exploding plane?'

'In the war,' said the man.

'I'd better tether her,' said Phryne, walking back to Rigel over meadow grass. 'Take this side, will you, and we'll peg down the wings.'

'I never heard of hobbling a plane,' said the man, fascinated. 'Will she take off and fly away herself, or does she get lonely for other planes?'

'Ground wind,' explained Phryne. 'She's fragile.' Running a gloved hand along the wings, she realized that each edge had been carrying a load of ice. She wondered how much longer she would have been able to fly if she hadn't found the ground. Not very long, she decided, and drove the tent-peg down hard into a crack in the rock. She had landed on alpine meadow, sweet-smelling and flowered, with only the occasional boulder showing through the blanket of herbs. Mount Howitt loomed. It looked very close. So close that Phryne shut her eyes for a moment, aware that she had been only a few minutes' flying time from a very permanent smash.

'I say, are you all right?' asked the Ancient Mariner. 'Sorry about collaring you like that. I thought that the plane would go up. Did I hurt you?'

He had completed the tying down of his wing and now came to support Phryne with a solicitous hand under her elbow. She opened her eyes and looked at him.

'A trustworthy face,' Dot had said. Under the bristling beard and the flowing hair, it was a strong, bony face with a heavy jawbone and a strong, solid skull. He had a broad nose, a wide mouth, and the most beautiful clear eyes of a shade between green and grey, speckled with golden flecks like sunlight on a trout stream. He was smiling uncertainly. Phryne smiled back.

'No, no, you didn't hurt me at all, and you would have saved my life if I had been carrying explosives or a lot more fuel. Quick thinking indeed! My name is Phryne Fisher.'

'I'm pleased to meet you,' he said as if he really meant it. 'Up here they call me Vic.'

'Nothing else? Just Vic?'

'Vic the hermit,' he explained. 'The cattlemen employ me in autumn to help with the muster. Otherwise I only see people when I go down to Talbotville for stores. This is a treat! But you must be cold, and you can't take off again while the mist is down. Would you like to come to my house?'

'Very kind of you, Mr. Freeman,' said Phryne.

The hand dropped away from the elbow. He stared at her, his face flattening into a mask. He was not the Ancient Mariner, Phryne realized, but the golden mask of an old Viking. She gathered her resources. She did not fancy going to this hermit's cave under false pretences.

'I've come to find you, Mr. Freeman, but I'll go away again as soon as the weather lifts. I don't want to ruin your solitude. In view of your history I perfectly understand it. But you cannot shut out the world altogether, you know. Some things have to be settled, after which I will go away and you can forget all about me, and the world, if you want to.'

He turned and walked away, hands clasped, until he was lost in the mist. Phryne sat down collectedly and groped for a cigarette, realized that her lighter was in the plane and delved for it. He was back before she had smoked half the gasper.

'I knew, I knew that someone would come eventually. I suppose I am lucky that it's you, Miss, Miss Fisher. What has happened? Is my father, my mother…'

'Your father is dead,' said Phryne gently. 'He died six months ago. Have you been receiving your mother's letters?'

'Yes, well, yes, I have been getting them, but I haven't been answering. She never cared for me, you know, and I thought that if I vanished it would give Charles a chance. How, how is Charles?'

'Charles is fine,' lied Phryne. 'He could not be said to be an excellent specimen of manhood, but so few are in these parlous times. He thought that you were dead.'

'Yes, that's what she told him. I wrote to my father a few times, but he kept wanting me to come back. I couldn't live in a city again. I couldn't! So I stopped writing to him, too. And I found a source of income on my own, and didn't need money any more. Poor Dad. She led him a dog's life. He'll be glad that it's over. Let's get off the plain, Miss Fisher, it'll snow soon, more than likely.'

'I asked Albert Stout what the weather would be like and he said it would be clear,' said Phryne rather indignantly as she unloaded her small case and the hamper from the plane. Vic chuckled, heaving the hamper up in his arms without effort.

'You should have asked him for the weather for the High Plains. In the valley it'll still be clear. He's never wrong, but you have to give him precise instructions. He isn't used to the idea of aeroplanes. Can't say that I am, either. How were you going to find me, Miss Fisher? I'm only up here because the packhorse slipped his head rope and I have to get him down before it gets too cold. Lucky loves mountain grass. And I got some yams, too. Good feed for a change.'

He whistled, and a very self-important dog came out of the fog, escorting a packhorse with an unusual gait.

'What is it, half kangaroo?' asked Phryne as the pony hopped forward with both front hoofs together.

'No, hobbled. He can cover a long distance like that, the rascal.'

The horse stood obediently while Vic unfastened the hobbles and slung the hamper, the case, and a sack onto its back. The dog sat with its paws precisely in line, radiating the consciousness of being a good dog.

'There. Now, off we go, before we freeze. Come on, Mack. Can you walk all right, Miss Fisher?'

'Suppose you call me Phryne and I'll call you Vic, eh? How far?'

'About a thousand feet,' said Vic, walking through the mist-shrouded wattle to the edge of what looked like a precipice. 'Not far. Watch your step, though.'

Phryne thanked the Lord that she was wearing boots and followed Vic down a boulder-strewn path, just wide enough for horse and man to walk abreast, which plunged in a swooping curve down the side of the High Plains. It was a strange journey. Trees higher than any she had ever seen soared up out of sight. She concentrated on her footing. The low cloud had produced silence, except for the rustle of unknown creatures in the undergrowth. All of her life had been spent in cities, or in the polite woods of England and the tamed bush of Melbourne. This cold wilderness was utterly unfamiliar, but it did not feel hostile, just indifferent to her fate. If she fell off this path and was broken into a hundred pieces nothing up here would be one whit interested. Phryne kept her eyes on the rocks and tried not to grab at passing trees. Leather was not the ideal medium for boot soles. Every surface appeared to be slippery. Already a little trickle of water was running down these stones. Phryne suspected that when it began to rain on the High Plains, the path would be the bed of a stream.

'Vic, slow down, I can't keep up,' she called in sudden panic as the packhorse rounded a bend and went out of sight. She heard him stop.

'Come up here to the front and take the bridle,' he said, and just the sound of another human voice was a relief. 'It is a bit difficult, but it's really hard going through the trees. Take it slowly, now, just edge around Lucky here. He won't kick.'

Phryne grabbed a tree branch and showered herself with icy water. She spluttered, swore, and found the rear of the horse by touch. There was not much room between the pony and the edge of the path, but she managed and the creature snuffled her companionably as she leaned around and took the bridle.

'We're halfway,' said Vic, pointing to a red sock tied to a low branch. 'That's my marker. Now we turn a little and then down again. Let the pony pick his way, Phryne, and you follow. He won't fall.'

Hanging onto another warm-blooded creature, which more-over appeared to know exactly what it was doing, did much to restore Phryne's confidence. The trees grew thicker, the path wandered across the face of the slope rather than going straight down it, and she had time to observe the change in the vegeta-tion. More wattle, past its bloom but bravely golden still, and scarves of mist caught in the olive-green leaves of snow gums. Decorated bark which looked as though it had been dyed; once the unmistakable shape of a scar showed that a bark dish had been cut from a very old tree.

'Did the Aborigines live here?' she asked.

Vic, further down, stopped. 'They didn't live here, they came here. Every year, November to January, the Brabiralung and the Yaimathang people, clans of the Kurnai.'

'They came here? Why?' asked Phryne. 'Surely the hunting would be better in the lowlands, and how did they manage the cold?'

'October is an odd month up here. Usually it's warm, but it can change like lightning. November's the beginning of summer, and it brings the Bogong moth.'

'The what moth?'

'Bogong. Agrotis Infusa, to be precise.' The cool, educated enunciation which Vic had been taught at school had never left him, and sounded very odd out here in primeval forest. 'It's a brown moth which aestivates in caves up here. In millions. The tribes used to walk up to eat all the Bogong moths they could catch and cook. Someone has cut a coolamon from that tree, as you noticed. But they never stayed. It was a truce time for the tribes—ordinarily they did not get on. Not far now. Mack!'

Phryne edged closer to the packhorse, holding on by the cheek-strap, as Mack the dog belted past, almost knocking her off her already uncertain feet. The path seemed to have no end. The mist made it impossible to see very far down, and Phryne felt that this was probably fortunate.

At last the slope became easier. Phryne let the horse have its head and it led her confidently down through virgin forest into a completely unsuspected clearing.

There was flat space, perhaps forty yards long and fifteen wide: a shelf where a large chunk of mountain had fallen off a few million years ago. It was green, clothed in soft, silvery grass, and it showed signs of habitation. Where a spring leapt down the crags, presumably the MacAlister Springs, a wooden tub had been built. A stable and a house, complete with outhouse, nestled back into the hill. They were made of grey timber, clinker-built, and roofed with carefully cut shingles. Two large tree-trunks lay across each roof, lashed down, and dotted with large stones. The clearing looked vaguely Swiss, certainly alpine, and was extremely welcome.

'Come in,' invited the hermit, pushing open a stout wooden door. Phryne stepped over the lintel into a large room. She walked to the fire and subsided in a heap in front of it, aware that she was dangerously cold.

Vic built up the fire with knots of what he called woollybut, until the flames leapt up the stone chimney, breathing heat in gusts like a dragon. He swung the kettle—hung on a stout, blackened iron hook and chain—over the fire, and went out to rub down and rehobble Lucky. Phryne began to thaw. As soon as she could feel her feet she got up and began to explore.

So this was the Old Bark Hut of song. Interesting. It was certainly a luxury version. It had floor-boards, for a start, where the original had probably had a dirt floor. The walls were thick, and lined with a fascinating collection of old newspapers. Useful, Phryne thought; if one ran out of books one could always read the walls. *Peace*, one headline said. The next proclaimed *Influenza Epidemic: New Government Measures*. Vic had built a lot of furniture. There was a tall cupboard against one wall, filled with books and papers. Phryne pulled out a stout red volume. *The Native Tribes of South Eastern Australia* by A. Howitt. Hmm. Was that the same Howitt of Mount Howitt? She expected that it was. How many Howitts could there be in east Gippsland? She scanned the books quickly. Botany, ethnology, famous travellers, children's books, John Buchan for adventure, the whole of Dickens for the winter. Another cupboard held tinned and preserved food, several cups and plates, salt and flour. The hermit's bed was a bunk, built into the wall, loaded with blankets and skin rugs. The only sign of Vic's old occupation was his army knapsack, with his name and rank still stencilled on it in white paint.

An axe, a twig broom, and miscellaneous rabbit snares hung on the wall, and several skinning knives were stuck into a block.

Phryne sat down in the easy chair, which had been carved from the bole and two branches of a gum, and cushioned with rabbit skins most beautifully tanned and finished. The room was lit by two windows, with rolled-up blinds and shutters. A kerosene lamp swung on a chain from the roof. The hut was clean, neat, and smelt refreshingly of pine.

Vic had made a chimney by collecting grey volcanic stones of a reasonably uniform size and gluing them together with mud. It seemed solid enough.

Phryne realized that her hands were sufficiently warm to take off her gloves, and was attempting to do so when Vic re-entered, carrying her hamper and suitcase and the sack.

'Can you help me?' she asked. 'My fingers won't work.' Vic knelt and eased off the sopping sheepskin until each glove was turned inside out. Phryne's fingers, she noticed, were still blue.

'Better get warm,' he commented, holding both of her hands easily in one warm clasp. 'What about your feet?'

Phryne allowed him to unlatch and remove her boots, and the two pairs of socks (one silk, one wool) underneath. He rubbed her toes back into a semblance of life.

'It must be very cold in the sky,' he said, putting down one foot and taking up the other. 'Is it always like this?'

'No, not at all. Not unless one is idiotic enough to fly over mountains and land in freezing fog. Compared to today, all previous cold has been pleasantly cool.'

'I've brought in all your baggage. Is there anything I can bring you? Sit and get warm.'

'Smelling-salts? No, I'm fine, getting warmer by the moment. A cup of tea would be heavenly. Tell me, Vic,' she gestured at the other massive chair, 'why did you build two chairs?'

'Why, in case I had visitors. I see a lot of people during the season, you know. Even up here I hear most of the news, and I can order books from Melbourne and stores from Talbotville. Stockmen drop in for a yarn occasionally, and one year three of them were bushed in the biggest snowstorm I've ever seen. We were unable to dig out past the stable for three days. Luckily I had enough stores, or we would have done a perish. Ah. Kettle's boiling. I'll just feed the dog and you shall have your tea, Miss, er, Phryne.'

He smiled an enchanting smile, extracted a rabbit carcass from the meat safe, and called Mack.

'What sort of dog is he?'

'Kelpie. Kelpie cross, I think. Black and White dog.' Vic reached an acceptable definition. 'Missus Anne gave him to me when he was a puppy. He's a good dog, anyway,' he added, giving the rabbit to Mack, who sensed that he was being complimented and wagged his tail. 'Take it outside, Mack, there's a good chap.'

Mack took the carcass in a firm grip and leapt out the window with it.

'He's showing off,' said Vic indulgently. 'Used to do that when snow was too high for him to get out the door.'

Phryne accepted the tea in a large china mug.

'There's no milk, but sugar's in that dish. Aren't many ants up this high. Would you like a rug? Are you still cold?'

'Yes, thank you.' Phryne wondered at the acclimatization of Vic, who was clad only in drill trousers and a flannel shirt. He tucked a large rabbit-fur rug around her.

'Lovely tanning. Did you do it?'

'Yes. I don't like hunting the native beasts, but rabbits are pests, and the skin cures easily. I need meat—I have to feed Mack. He can hunt for himself as long as there isn't too much snow, but the weather's late this year.'

'How about Lucky?'

'I bring up a bag of oats and some beans when I bring the stores, and he can graze. It's thin grass up this high, but it's good.'

'There's something...large, under your bunk,' said Phryne. This was not what she had been intending to say. The bunk creaked. Vic laughed. He rummaged in the sack and scattered a handful of bright yellow daisies with roots on the floor, and whistled. It was a carrying, pleasant, bird-like whistle. The thing under the bunk heaved forward, blinked at the light, and sniffed loudly, as a pig will.

'It's a wombat!' cried Phryne with delight. 'I've never seen one close before!'

'That's Wom. I've had him since he was a little 'un. He must have lost his mother. He isn't really big yet. Come on, Wom, old man, come and meet the lady.'

He heaved the creature along the floor, gave it another handful of daisies, and Phryne patted her first wombat. He was a stocky, faintly belligerent animal, with black boot-button eyes and stumpy legs. He stood with his front feet on the edge of the skin rug and champed, allowing Phryne to stroke his thick, deep fur and run her hands along his muzzle and up to the round, furry ears. He had bristly black whiskers as strong as cobbler's thread.

'Pretty thing,' murmured Phryne. 'Aren't you lovely?'

Wom finished the daisy roots and stumped back across the floor and under the bunk. The show was over.

'You see why I can't go back to the city, don't you?' asked Vic.

Phryne surveyed the cosy hut and listened to the wombat eating the last of his daisies. Faintly, as though it was far away, she heard the song of a thrush, and the shuffle of horse-hoofs shifting as Lucky grazed.

'Yes,' she said gravely. 'I see.'

Chapter Fourteen

*NICKY: It's funny how Mother's generation
always longed to be old when they were young,
and we strain every nerve to keep young.*

*BUNTY: That's because we can see what's
coming so much more clearly.*

The Vortex, Noel Coward

'It will be dark soon,' Vic observed. 'Come and have a look at the mountains. The mist has lifted a bit.'

Phryne dragged on her stiff boots and wrapped her rug, toga-fashion, around her shoulders. She had been soundly beaten at chess, which did not surprise her, and had absorbed an interesting soup made of native yams, onions, and other ingredients which she had not identified and about which she did not want to enquire. That delicate, fish-like flesh—was it indeed fish, or was it possibly snake? Much better not to know. She found a safety pin in her case to secure the rug, and followed her host out of the hut and along the cleared space to view the prospect.

'Oh, Lord,' she breathed, standing back from a precipice.

'Mount Howitt,' said Vic, pleased with the response. 'That is the Cross-Cut Saw, beneath it is the Terrible Hollow where the Wonnangatta is born, somewhere down in the depths. See how deep it is? Those are the very tops of snow gums you can see along the edge. That's Mount Speculation, and next to it, the Viking.'

It was beautiful country, with a terrible, cold, geometric precision. A god with a strange sense of humour had carved the serrations in the Cross-Cut Saw, knowing that men would come to harvest and spoil the forest, and sometimes pay for it with their lives. Olive leaves, grey rocks, pale sky, silver kangaroo grass speckled with little points of colour that were alpine flowers. And at her feet a drop of a thousand feet, straight down.

'Why did they come here?' she asked, speaking to herself. 'Why on earth did men come here? They aren't wanted.'

'Not so much not wanted, just not noticed. You could hide an army in that valley, and no one would know. This is a dangerous place, Phryne, and I fell in love with danger. I came here broken, half destroyed—damaged, as I thought, beyond repair. I came, I came without any expectations at all; just the need to get away from men, chattering, murdering monkeys. You don't know what it was like. You know about me, don't you? You've researched me. But you don't know about Pozières.'

'Well, yes, I do, I spoke to some friends of mine who were there. They were right, too. They said that Pozières would have done for you, as it did for them.'

'What happened to them?' asked Vic, staring out into the blue haze of further mountains beyond the Viking.

'They were wounded; one was wounded and the other developed soldier's heart, and they were sent home.'

'They were lucky.'

'They know. They said that Pozières was worse than Gallipoli.'

'Pozières was like hell. I couldn't hear after the first twelve hours. I mean, I couldn't hear voices, but inside my head the big guns fired incessantly. They never stopped, not for a moment, not while I slept or ate, always a creeping barrage getting closer and closer, and the crump and the flash of H. E. every time I closed my eyes. I shook as though I had malaria. The vibrations and shock had entered my bones. I wanted to die, but it seemed too easy just to die.'

Vic was talking eagerly now, as though the words had been pent inside him for a long time, never spoken, not even to himself, the dog, or the mountains.

'When I got home, I couldn't hear what people said over the big guns. I knew I had to get away; actually, I came here to die. I felt that I couldn't just up and kill myself in my mother's house. There was Charlie to consider, you know. Then, it was the most astounding thing, Phryne. I came up here on foot, with just a tent and some gear, and the gun I meant to use, and I was so tired after the climb that I decided to wait until dawn. I didn't even pitch the tent, just lay down in the grass next to the springs. I fell asleep because I was so tired. I used to get dreadfully tired then, and when I woke up I heard the water; the stream running over the rocks and singing. It took me a moment to realize where I was and what had changed, and then I knew that the guns were silent. They had just stopped. I lay there and listened to the water for the whole day, just the sound of falling water. I never heard a sweeter song. I was afraid to sleep, in case it came back, the noise and the shaking. But I did sleep, and I woke again with a terrible cold from lying in wet grass and still just the noise of water. I put up my tent and lit a fire and sneezed a lot and I was perfectly happy for the first time in my life. Then I went down the mountain again, bought some stores, and sent a message to the leaseholder asking if I could stay. He didn't mind me.'

'Then what did you do?'

'The stockmen helped me. They were a bit wary at first, but when they realized that I wasn't going to make trouble and I showed them I could ride, they came to the conclusion that I was a good chap. Bit strange perhaps, but not a cattle thief or a mad hunter, and they showed me how to build a log hut. They build them, you know, each family, for the muster. They gave me a lot of tips. It took me all summer to get it right—you have to build the chimney first, as I found when my first effort burned down. I got it right the second time. They know about what you can eat from the bush; there's no need to starve here as long as you have your wits about you. And I got handouts from Dad and bought luxuries, like jam and books and tobacco and the occasional bottle of brandy. And it's a very comfortable hut, don't you think?'

'Palatial,' agreed Phryne. 'Do you know the ladies in Talbotville? Anne Purvis and Josephine Binet. I asked Miss Binet why she lived there and she showed me the mountains. It seemed reasonable. I have never seen such beautiful scenery.'

'It's more than the scenery. The people have an exquisite delicacy which astonished me. I was dreading a barrage of questions, but no one asked me any. They are rough fellows, to be sure, but the most anyone has ever said in my hearing was that they s'posed I had a bad war. Quite true. But it was almost worth it. If it hadn't happened I would have just stayed in the city, been incompetent at business, and been halfway happy.'

'You might have married and had children,' commented Phryne.

'Yes, I suppose so. And made some poor woman miserable. I'll never marry now. I'm too used to my own company. Old Mr. Treasure sold me Lucky. Said that he was the only neddy he'd ever met who hated other horses. "He's a cross-grained cuss," he said, "so I reckon you'll match." And we do.'

'I don't find you cross-grained.' Phryne smiled up into the trout-stream eyes. 'You have been very kind to me, seeing that I dropped in on you out of the sky and broke your solitude into bits.'

He did not answer at once, but took her hand consideringly.

'If anyone had to break it, I am glad it was you,' he said.

Phryne was a little disconcerted. This was a man who, on his own admission, had been completely loopy for almost a year. On the other hand, he was now extremely sane, and strong, and gentle. She gave the hand a squeeze and released herself.

'I must get back from this edge,' she said. 'I don't like heights.'

'You don't like heights! What about that plane?'

'That's different.' Phryne retreated until she could sit down on the grass a good ten yards from the precipice. 'You don't feel the ground pulling you down in a plane. I'll show you tomorrow. I'll take you for a ride, if you like.'

'Perhaps,' said Vic dubiously. 'I'll think about it.'

Phryne was conducted on a tour of the rest of the manor. Lucky the horse, on neck-rope and long line, grazed contentedly. He was provided with a very comfortable stable, complete with manger, soundly padded with bark against draughts. Alpine hay cushioned the floor.

'Look at this,' said Vic, lifting away a wisp of grass. 'I found them yesterday and moved Lucky's feed into the other crib, in case he disturbed them.'

In a woven, cup-shaped nest, such as a bird might make, were three small baby creatures of some sort, their heads visible through the slit in their mother's pouch. She opened one eye at the light, then closed it again as Vic's shadow blocked the sun.

'What are they?' asked Phryne, as the babies uttered little squeaks and dived into their pouch.

Vic covered the mother again before he replied. 'Flying possums. I can't imagine why she chose to live in the hay, they are supposed to live in tree-hollows. But there is no accounting for possums.'

Phryne observed that the creature had long grey fur, unlike the short dark velvet of lowland possums. Obviously an adaptation against the cold. For no reason Phryne was suddenly reminded of the problem she had left unsolved in the city. Charles had been released and gone back (presumably) to his mother. She would tell him that Phryne had gone in search of Vic. And what of Nerine? Phryne found that she regarded all of them with weary indifference. Who cared what happened to any of them? Except, of course, the delectable Tintagel Stone. Phryne came out of the stable to inspect the wooden tub which Vic had constructed to dam the waters of the MacAlister Springs on its way down the mountain. Next to the tub was a curious sort of sieve. Phryne picked it up.

'What's this?' she asked idly, struck with a disconcertingly sensual image of Tintagel Stone. Vic took it out of her hands.

'Oh, nothing. Just a sieve.'

'Oh, nothing?' mocked Phryne, releasing the image reluctantly. 'You don't haul artefacts twenty miles up the mountain for nothing. You do not strike me as a frivolous man, Vic.'

Vic said nothing. Phryne inspected the thing again.

'Aha!' she said. 'I have seen something like this before. What is your source of income, eh? Enough to give you books and onions and a packhorse?'

'You've guessed,' admitted Vic, 'but for God's sake promise that you won't tell anyone.' He grasped Phryne by the upper arms and she shook herself free irritably.

'Of course I won't tell anyone. What do you take me for? And don't lay hands on me unless I ask you to!'

Green eyes flashed, black hair flew as she shook her head. Vic stepped back a pace.

'Sorry.'

'So, you found gold. I should have guessed. Alluvial gold, the book said. But I thought it had all run out.'

'Not run out, just uneconomical to dig and transport. It was down Crooked River and Black Snake Creek way that they made the big strikes: Pioneer Reef, Star of Australia. But almost all of the little creeks have some gold in them. I found it entirely by accident, I was experimenting with making vellum. There is a receipt for it in one of the Settler's Handbooks. Useful ideas they have sometimes, though their Supreme Mousetrap does not work, I tried it.'

'What did it trap?'

'Me, mostly. I decided I needed my fingers and could establish a reasonable compromise with the mice. Anyway, I laid a sheepskin in the tub, fleece up, for a week, and when I took it out to work it...'

'It was a golden fleece,' Phryne laughed. 'How very classical.'

'Yes. That is how they trapped water-borne gold in Jason's day, I imagine. I dried the fleece (ruining my vellum experiment) and shook it out over a cloth, and I had a small amount of pure gold. I took it down to Talbotville, swore Albert Stout to secrecy, and sent the package to the assayer in the city. He buys it at currency prices. The sieve does the same as the sheepskin but lets the water through better. I don't want to interrupt the flow of the springs more than I can help, especially in the summer, and in the winter the spate of ground-water is too great. But in spring and autumn I can catch enough gold to keep myself in luxury. It was so providential, Phryne. I felt that the mountains had no objection to me, that they didn't mind if I stayed, that in fact they were encouraging me to stay, as though I was accepted. Do you see? That's why I don't want anyone to know. Times are getting tough in the city. If it were known that there was gold here, the place would be flooded with miners digging up the bush, cutting down the trees, murdering each other. Men will do anything for gold. Do you see?'

His face was still a mask, the eyes anxious. Phryne put her arms around his neck.

'Of course I see, and no one will ever know from me. I promise,' she said, and kissed him. His mouth was warm and his embrace strong as his arms closed around her. She heard his heart beating under her cheek, fast as a trip-hammer.

'You promise?' he whispered.

'I promise,' she replied. This time the kiss lasted for longer, and she slid her hands down his muscular back. He gasped.

'Come inside,' she suggested. 'It's getting cold, and we need to talk. I did not come here to seduce you,' she added. 'I would not take advantage of you. Come on. I have all sorts of goodies in that hamper which I haven't even opened.'

One of the goodies she had brought along was her diaphragm. One never knew.

Charles Freeman, released and vengeful, was in Dargo post office, trying to get the postmaster to pay attention.

'It's a place called Talbotville,' he said urgently. 'I need to get there right away!'

'You'll need a riding horse,' said the postmaster indifferently. He did not like the look of Charles. The young man was dishevelled and exuded an air of panic which the postmaster instinctively distrusted.

'Isn't there a bus or something?'

'Bus? There isn't even a road, just the packhorse track. You sure you want to go to Talbotville? There's even less there to interest a city chap like you than here in Dargo.'

Charles looked at Dargo from the post office door. It was a dilapidated place; it looked half-built. It seemed to have been constructed on the ruins of a larger town. Houses were falling into disrepair. His bed in the pub had been cold and vaguely damp, and the drovers carousing under him had not let him sleep. The publican's wife had served him a slab of steak the size of his hand for breakfast, with two fried eggs that had stared up into his queasy face. The only coffee in Dargo came out of a bottle marked 'Coffee and Chicory Essence,' and he was scared by the rough men and the slatternly women. He wanted desperately to go back to Melbourne, where they understood civilization. However, he had a mission. His mother had made that clear. Unless he completed it he would lose all the position and wealth he held dear. So he persisted.

'Where can I hire a horse?' he asked the local policeman.

The hamper proved to contain a fruit cake—freshly baked, and sewn in its baking tin into a canvas cover—a goodly portion of a ham, a loaf of new white bread, a pound of butter, two tins of condensed milk and several other tins, a tin opener, knives and forks and spoons and plates, a tin of tea and one of the dark Italian espresso coffee that Phryne favoured, a camping kettle and a spirit stove, a bottle of methylated spirits that was carefully sealed in oilskin, and the box of Hillier's chocolates.

'Game soup.' Phryne was reading the labels of the tins. 'Tomatoes, and this one is apricots. What a feast, eh?'

Vic stared at the food spread out on the floor.

'I would never have bought all this luxury stuff,' he said. 'I couldn't justify loading poor old Lucky with chocolates and coffee. Coffee! I haven't tasted it in years. And milk! I really miss milk. I thought of having a milking nanny-goat but they're herd animals and she'd be lonely, and also she might get away. Goats destroy the bush. What's in that padded box?'

'Eggs,' said Phryne, investigating. 'Only one broken. It's getting dark, so I'll just slip out to the outhouse. Back in a tick. If I'm not, send out a search party,' she added, rummaging in her own little case for a certain appliance.

The privy was spotlessly kept and provided with newspaper cut into neat squares and threaded onto a string. It was getting dark, and cold, and the silence was beginning to get to Phryne. It was not the absence of sound such as is produced by ear-plugs. It was the silence of great emptiness, in which all sorts of small lives were pursuing their way in the centre of a space so huge that the sounds of their living and dying did not impinge at all.

Something screamed in the valley. Phryne jumped, told herself firmly that it was a bird, and re-entered the cabin just short of a run.

Vic had piled up the fire with knotted logs, which produced a bright flame. Phryne took off her boots and her flying suit, and sat down on the warmed boards dressed in her long woollies and her rug. She wished that she had thought to bring a dress. Vic looked down at her and thought that she looked delicate and strong, with her limbs clad only in sensible red flannel and the rug falling from her straight shoulders over the small, well-defined breasts. He caught his breath. She tilted her head, the black hair flicking aside from green eyes.

'We must talk,' she insisted. 'What's for dinner?'

He lit the kerosene lamp and it shed a soft golden light. Phryne, used to the white glare of electricity, was pleased by this glow that produced no sharp shadows.

'Ham omelette,' he said gravely. 'Madame will be pleased to enjoy game soup. Bread and butter. Irish coffee. Chocolates.

The staff have hay, raw rabbit, and potatoes. Put a spud on the floor, Phryne, for Wom.'

Phryne got up and extracted a potato from the net hung high on a rafter, and placed it solemnly beside her. Vic said hurriedly, 'Not behind you! Put it in front of you!'

But it was too late. Something as stocky and as strong as a tank rumbled out from under the bunk at a fast trot and went straight through Phryne as though she wasn't there. Wom had smelt his favourite food and was not to be deflected by a mere human in his path. Phryne went down, trodden underpaw, laughing help-lessly. Then, before she could gather herself together again, she was flattened for a second time by the return journey. Wom, spud held firmly in strong jaws, retired under the bunk to eat in privacy.

'Sorry, Phryne. Are you all right?' asked Vic, observing her shoulders to be shaking. 'He didn't hurt you, did he?' Vic was reassured by Phryne's laughter. 'Wombats go directly for their target. Nothing bothers them, and they are very strong. If you are in the way you get mowed down like grass.'

'What if there was a wall in the way?' Phryne asked, feeling her thighs for bruises. Vic laughed.

'Wouldn't make any difference. He'd just barge through it. I can tell I will be busy making doors when he's bigger.'

'What if they can't break through? If the barrier is a rock, say, or a tree?'

'They'll dig under, they can dig like badgers. The one thing they won't do is turn aside.'

'He's faster than he was before.' Phryne decided that she had sustained no lasting damage.

'It's night. He's nocturnal. He only came out in the light because he loves those daisy roots. But he dotes on potatoes. Can't imagine why, because he would definitely not find them in the wild. I found out one day when I was making soup. I used to keep the spuds in a sack. Once he'd had a taste of the peel he went directly to the sack, bit straight through double hessian, and demolished pounds of them before I rescued the rest and hung them on a rafter. He hasn't tried to get them there.'

'Lucky he hasn't noticed them, or he'd have demolished the house. That smells good.'

'Dinner is served,' said Vic, helping Phryne to her feet and pulling out a chair at the table. '*Bon appetit.*'

Charles Freeman found the livery stable, and a man who smelt disagreeably of horses informed him that a pack-train was going to Talbotville on the morrow, starting at 5 a.m. Charles felt faint. What an hour! The man eyed him cynically.

'Yair, we can hire you a neddy. You a good rider?'

Charles had ridden extensively in the park and considered himself a master of the equestrian arts. He drew himself up.

'Yes, I am a good rider,' he snapped.

'Well, we got just the moke for yer.' The man spat, perilously close to Charles' highly polished shoes. 'You got any riding gear?'

'Only what I'm wearing.'

The stableman surveyed Charles. Quiet grey suit as worn, white shirt wilting at the collar, city shoes. He grunted.

'Better get on over to the store and get some moleskins and a pair of boots. You can't ride in that.'

'I shall ride as I please.' Charles flounced out of the stable. Impudent hayseed! These clothes were very fashionable and had sufficed for riding with the best people. He had not thought that the bush had such nice tastes.

Now he must order that awful woman to wake him early enough to join the packhorse train, since this looked to be the only way he was going to get to Talbotville. And he had to get to Talbotville because he had to find Vic.

'Now, shall we talk?' asked Phryne, breathing in the bracing scent of coffee and brandy, undefiled with the condensed milk Vic had poured into his. She looked at him. The long hair was corn-coloured and fell down over his shoulders to his chest. His beard was, Phryne knew, soft; not the bedsprings she had previously been close to, worn by young artists in search of Bohemia. His eyes were calm, but they glowed.

'Yes. What shall we talk about first?'

'The legal angle. Your father has left you his house and his money. He has left the business to Charles. What do you want to do about the inheritance?'

'I don't want it,' he said, faintly surprised that she had to ask. 'I don't want any of it. I don't want to see my mother again, and I don't really want to see Charles again, either, though I wish him well. There must be some sort of legal way I can refuse the bequest.'

'You really don't want it? It's a lot of money.'

'What would I do with a lot of money?' he asked, smiling. 'I am an immeasurably wealthy man. If I had to go back to Melbourne I would never recover from my poverty.'

'You are sure?'

'Yes, I am sure.'

'Good. I have this paper that a lawyer friend drew up for me. It repudiates the inheritance. But...'

'Where do I sign?'

'Not so fast. If you sign it, you will have no further claim on your father's estate. What if you get sick, can't stay here? What if you break a leg or something, miscalculating Wom's trajectory?'

'Misses Anne and Jo will look after me, and then I'll come back here. I will die here,' he said quietly. 'I will never go back. Have you got a pen?'

Phryne supplied her own fountain-pen and watched him sign his full name, Victor Ernest Freeman. She signed underneath as a witness. Vic opened the cupboard and showed Phryne a savings-book. She read the balance and swore.

'Gold?'

'Gold. I don't need money. That's why I haven't panned for years. I built it up, bit by bit, until I had enough, then I let it be. Someone else might come after me and make the same discovery. I do not want to plunder the place. Well, that's my inheritance gone, thank God. More coffee?'

Phryne folded the paper and put it in her suitcase.

'Well, I have done what I came to do. Your mother hired me to find you and I found you. She was in a flap about the house and the money and you have solved that at one stroke of the pen. Now I can leave.'

'But not just now.'

'No. Not just now.'

Silence fell. The fire crackled. Mack the dog chased rabbits in his sleep, paws twitching. Outside it was black night. Phryne noticed that two things she had expected to see were missing.

'No clock, and no gun,' she commented.

'I hate clocks. They tick. Other things make noises in their time and need, but clocks mechanically beat the seconds to death. No clocks. I don't need one, anyway. I had a gun when I came here. I told you that, didn't I? When the noise in my head stopped, I didn't need it any more. I broke it, and threw it away. I was a soldier and had to carry a gun, once. Now I am a free man I will never carry a gun again. I snare my rabbits with wire slipnooses; they're killed instantly. And rabbits are the only things that I intend to kill.'

'I am concerned,' began Phryne, reaching a hand out of her wrappings to the man opposite her, 'I am concerned that by coming here I have broken your peace. And I am very concerned by the thought that if I make love with you, dear Vic, I will smash your solitude to pieces. You have lived without women all this time and felt no lack of them. Is it a good idea to waken all those sleeping desires? Won't you burn, once I am gone? For I shall go,' she added. 'I could not live here. The silence unsettles me. I like cities.'

He thought about it, stroking her hand very gently.

'I have burned,' he agreed. 'There was a girl in France, a real Mademoiselle from Armentières, and a nurse in England. I have not lost…my manhood. I would rather bear the pain, Phryne, than never to have known you at all.'

'You are sure?' she asked, and he nodded.

'I am sure.'

She stripped off the red flannel woollies, retaining her rug, and curled up in the bunk, watching him undress. A broad chest and wide shoulders were revealed as the checked shirt was peeled off; narrow waist and strong, thick thighs as the moleskins dropped. He moved with assurance as he threw back the coverings and climbed into his bed, and Phryne slid down between him and the wall and encircled him in her white arms.

He was uncertain at first, perhaps remembering other flesh, perhaps afraid of hurting her. They grew warmer and closer, coffee-flavoured breaths mingled. Long hair tickled her face as his beard scratched and his mouth found the right place.

If she cried out in ecstasy, pinned pleasurably as prey under a lion's paw, the golden hair about her face, who but the mountains was there to hear her?

Chapter Fifteen

*But you found the bush was dismal and a land
of no delight*

'In Defence of the Bush,' Banjo Paterson

Charles bumped painfully on the ridge-like back of a mean,
fly-bitten, grey stallion, which, he was convinced, the stableman
had allotted him out of pure envy. The beast was two-paced,
with a bone-shattering trot, a habit of biting at its rider's foot
if it got the chance, and with a mouth as hard as boiled leather,
almost impossible to control. Fortunately, it liked other horses
almost as much as it hated humans, and was pleased to walk
along behind the packhorse train, trying to wipe Charles off
against passing rocks in absent-minded malice.

The landscape did not please him. It was all so uncontrolled.
No one had planted all these trees and all that thick understorey
scrub; it had just been allowed to grow wherever it liked. The
track was hardly encouraging either. It was disagreeably stony
and uneven, and his mount, Charles saw with pleasure, was
having a certain difficulty in negotiating it. He wished that the
creature would break several legs.

The pack-train, tethered loosely nose to tail, left traces as
they passed; fresh dung that steamed. Charles wrinkled his
nose. Animals were so…animalistic. He was convinced that at

Talbotville he would be lucky to find a hotel, and very lucky indeed if dinner did not consist of tough steak with two fried eggs.

His mount stumbled, and he swore as he dragged at its head. Before he left the city, he had had a pleasant, romantic view of the bush: out there somewhere, brave women and strong men. Now he was convinced that he hated every line Banjo Paterson had ever written, and determined that once he had concluded his task he would never, never come back.

◇◇◇

Phryne woke, warm and assuaged, with the conviction that her hair had turned gold overnight. She tugged at a tress of it, eliciting a sleepy murmur from the man next to her under the rabbit skins, and remembered that she had seduced a hermit. Her recollections of the night were extremely agreeable, and she closed her eyes and snuggled into Vic's embrace.

'Mmm?' he murmured interrogatively. 'Phryne,' he concluded, identifying her to his satisfaction. 'Oh Phryne, my dear.'

Phryne decided that although it was morning, at least morning enough to distinguish black hair from gold, and although this was a tough country, requiring all its citizens to be up and doing, she did not need to be up and doing anything just yet.

She was drowsing into sleep again when the man beside her convulsed and swore.

'Damn! Sorry, Phryne, that was Mack. He wakes me up like that if he thinks I've overslept.'

'Wakes you how?' She was interested in what part of Vic Mack had evidently bitten.

'He pushes his great wet cold nose in my ear. I'll just let him out.'

'I'll go out, too, if I can find my boots.'

She found the boots, donned them with difficulty—they had dried into unfootlike shapes—and pulled on her woollies and the rug. Sun flooded into the little house as Vic opened the door. Mack bounced out into the clearing, barked at a flying parrot, which surely could not have been black, and trotted off to the springs for a drink. Phryne joined him, and splashed her face with water so nearly gelid that she was stunned with cold.

'Snow water,' commented Vic, bare-chested in the thin sunlight. 'You've brought summer with you,' he said delightedly, and splashed enthusiastically, washing his face and chest.

Phryne, who had retreated out of the way of this exuberant hygiene, watched him in awe. Ice-water ran off him, almost steaming. His hair and beard shone in the bright light. He was a giant from the beginning of the world.

She pulled herself together. He was a perfectly ordinary hermit in moleskins that had seen better days, and his colouring had come from some remote Scandinavian ancestor.

He was, nonetheless, very impressive.

The forest exhaled, breathing fern and water scents. An eagle, ranging out from the cliffs, circled effortlessly overhead. Phryne went to sit down on the step, lighting a gasper and smoking luxuriously. The sun struck silver from the dewy grass, in which Mack rolled, making swathes of green where he had flattened the turf. Paradise, Phryne thought, blowing smoke rings. Paradise. It was only as she was called in to breakfast by the scent of buttered toast that she remembered that paradise always had a resident snake.

Charles had reached Talbotville about dusk, after following what seemed to be innumerable ridges, all marked carelessly with the occasional sock or cairn to suggest that there were tracks in the trackless hills. He was very tired, sore, bruised in his person by the badly maintained saddle and the unaccustomed exercise. There was, as he feared, only one hotel, if it could be dignified with such a name, and the stone-faced woman who served him dinner did indeed offer only steak and eggs. He ate it, because he was hungry. The packhorse train had been greeted by two frumpy women, a stout party in a suit with watch-chain, and a gaggle of uninteresting townsfolk and several dirty children. He sat in the public bar after mangling his way through the steak, as there was nowhere else to sit, and listened to the conversation of the stockmen.

'What's the news, then?' asked one, and the whiskered publican announced, 'We've only had a sheila in an aeroplane drop in on us!'

'No! You been drinking your own licker, Jim, you'll be seeing joe blakes on bicycles next!'

A general laugh. It appeared that the publican's liquor was generally suspect. Charles nursed his glass of beer.

'No, fair dinkum. We all saw her. A lady, it was. You know about it, mate, you brought up the fuel for the plane.'

'Oh, is that what all them drums was? A plane? Jeez.'

'Yair, and Dave's gonna get one too!' The publican laughed. 'Our Dave was real struck on her. Bit of all right, she was. Thin, with black hair. Funny name, now what was it? Phryne. That was the name. Miss Phryne Fisher. Couldn't she fly the thing, but! Dropped her onto the strip we cleared along the river as sweet as a bird.'

'What was she doin' here?' asked the packhorse man, draining his glass at a gulp. 'Another one, Jim.'

'She came to find...well, I reckon she came to find Vic. The ladies seemed sure that she didn't mean him no harm. And they made her promise not to try and take him back to the city. They said she came to tell him his father's dead.'

'Poor Vic,' commented Dave. 'As if he ain't had enough, to sic some sheila onto him.'

'She was all right, Missus Anne said she was all right. They wouldn't of told her if they hadn't thought she was,' insisted the publican. 'Promised she'd be back.'

'Yair, she promised to give me a ride in the plane,' grinned Dave. 'I'm gonna be in that! Reckon she's a good goer.'

'The sheila or the plane?' asked a grizzled stockman drily.

'The plane. She was a lady,' stated Dave firmly.

Charles was furious. It appeared that Phryne had stolen a march on him. He knew her ways; she'd have his poor mad brother crawling at her feet in a few minutes. He was sickened by all women, their smell and their lust. Well, he'd show her. He'd show both of them. It now appeared that Vic was not only not dead but definitely alive and living on the High Plains.

'Excuse me,' he interrupted the conversation. 'I'm Vic's brother, Charles. Can anyone take me to him? I have to see him.'

The whole population of the pub surveyed Charles in silence.

'You?' asked Dave finally. 'You're Vic's brother? You don't look like him.'

His voice held quiet contempt. Charles flushed with rage.

'Here's our photograph. It was taken before he went to the war,' he added. 'I was at school then.'

The photograph was passed around the pub, each man taking the time to study it profoundly. There was Vic, right enough, perfectly recognizable even with short hair and no beard. The eyes were the same. He was wearing a uniform. Next to him was a younger and smaller version of this same man, a little chubby, schoolboyish, but the same. On the back of the photo was written in Vic's flowing hand, 'To my brother Charlie with love from Vic.' It was conclusive.

'Yair, you're his brother all right. What makes you think he wants to see you?'

'I'm his brother!'

'Yair, you said that,' the old man pointed out.

Silence again.

'I'll pay you,' Charles said proudly. The air in the small pub seemed to congeal. He realized that he had said the wrong thing, and backtracked hastily.

'For your time, you know,' he babbled into cold silence.

'I'll take yer,' said Dave, having pity on him. 'But not for money. And if Vic don't want to see yer I'll take yer away again. We start in the morning. A quid will cover the stores.'

Charles passed over a pound.

'How long will it take?' he quavered. Dave considered.

'Two days, maybe three. Depends on the weather. Better see if Mrs. Plumpton has a spare oilskin. We'll have to ford the Wonnangatta River.'

'Isn't there a bridge?' asked Charles foolishly of the empty space where Dave had been. He flinched under the massed eyes, and went to the front of the pub to see if he could buy an oilskin from the publican's wife.

Anne Purvis strode into the house, flung down her armload of firewood and yelled, 'Jo! Wake up!'

'What?' came a voice from the centre of the big bed. Anne slapped at a lump where she guessed her friend's posterior might be. Jo emerged angrily.

'I've been up all night writing. Can't you indulge your diseased sense of rustic humour somewhere else?'

'Listen, this is important. A bloke came in with the packhorses today, reckons he's Vic's brother. Didn't say anything about it, mind, until he heard the others discussing Miss Phryne's visit and the plane and all.'

'What's he like?' asked Josephine, gathering up her wits and locating her boots and her skirt and dragging them on. Anne's brow was furrowed.

'I don't like the look of him, Jo. He's a plump, weak-looking little bloke with a permanent sneer. He don't look at all like Vic. If I fancied men, I'd fancy Vic; he's like one of them Vikings you were telling me about. Vic loves the bush. I don't reckon this bloke has ever been out here before, and you can tell he hates it.'

'Well? What's happened?'

'Young Dave's agreed to take him to Mac Springs,' said Anne. Josephine reflected.

'I don't think he can do Vic much harm, Anne. Not with Dave there. He was bound to happen along, I suppose. Pity Dave agreed, though. Why did he?'

'Missus Plumpton says Dave was sorry for him. He offered them all money to take him to Vic.'

'That was unwise. He certainly isn't used to bush ways, is he? I don't think we need to worry too much, Anne dear, but I might have a word with Dave. Put the kettle on. When are they setting out?'

'In the morning,' said Anne, slamming the cast-iron kettle onto the colonial stove. 'But I don't like it, Jo, I don't like this at all.'

'Neither do I,' agreed Josephine. 'I'll make the tea. You go out and get Dave.'

Phryne had spent a delightful day lazing in the sun, playing fetch with Mack (whose energy was awesome), making love in the kangaroo grass, and, as dusk approached, combing Vic's beautiful hair into a plait.

'It gets into my face and I sneeze,' she explained. He sat patiently under her hands, not wincing when the comb pulled. With the long hair out of the way, the planes of his face were visible, strong and flat. She kissed the triangle of white skin between the beard and the plait.

'Lovely. Many a maiden would pine for such hair. You don't resemble your brother at all, you know.'

'Mum reckoned I was a throwback to my dad's ancestors. They came from Norway, six generations back. How about rabbit stew for supper?'

Phryne suppressed the information that this would be the first rabbit she had eaten since her impoverished childhood. She reflected that she had sworn never to eat underground mutton again, informed herself that most promises were piecrust, and smiled.

'Good,' she said.

Dave and Charles had left Talbotville well supplied and in good weather, and the tracks were clear, at least to Dave. His ears still stung with the dressing down he had been given by Missus Jo, and the warnings about what she would do to him if any harm came to Vic. But as his employer groaned and shifted in a perfectly comfortable stock saddle, and almost toppled out of it, although he was held in so securely by the horns that a baby could have slept in it, he could not see that this poor townie could be any threat to Vic. Vic was a good bloke, a strong bloke, used to the bush and all its ways. A bit strange, living on his own in the high mountains. This city chap could never pose a threat to Vic. He didn't look well, either. He had not taken to sleeping on the ground, and he had caught a cold crossing the Wonnangatta. They were making good progress, though. The weather was fine, not too hot and not wet, and two days out they were already climbing up to the ridge which would take them onto the Cross-Cut Saw and round to Howitt Plains and down to Mac Springs. Dave shook his head. Well, tomorrow, perhaps late today if the weather held, he could deliver this palpitating incompetent to Vic and see what Vic wanted to do with him.

'Not far now,' he encouraged. 'We'll be out in the open in a tick, and you'll be able to see all across the Barry Ranges.'

'Oh, good,' said Charles with weak sarcasm.

'Yair, it's a beauty view,' agreed Dave innocently. Charles sat up straighter in the saddle and sighed.

Three days, Phryne had given herself, and the third was drawing on toward dusk. Vic was chopping wood. She watched him as he flexed his back, muscles rippling, and dropped the axe in exactly the right place, so that the wood split perfectly. He tossed the mound of logs onto his woodpile. Phryne embraced him, smelling the sharp scent of male human and sweat.

'I'll go tomorrow,' she said calmly. 'I have promised to be back in a week. It's been so lovely that I forgot the time. But I have to go, Vic.'

'And you won't be back?' he asked, hands closing on her shoulders.

'No, I don't think I should, do you?'

'I suppose not. Would you, if I couldn't live without you?'

'Of course.'

'I'll write,' he said. 'We'll see. One more night, Phryne. That shall be enough. Would you like to feed Mack? There's a rabbit in the Coolgardie. And I might give Lucky a bit of a rub down. He's been rolling in wet grass again. I don't want him to come down with colic.'

Phryne went into the house and was almost knocked down by Mack, whose knowledge of the English language encompassed words like 'feed' and 'rabbit.'

She realized that she wanted to leave, to go back to bright lights and noise and people and telephones and motor cars. The silence, which had healed Vic, was cumulative. She was now more, not less, frightened of the night than she had been when she arrived. She found herself singing loudly. Occasionally, although a warm sleeping man lay beside her, she woke in the dark, terrified by the thudding of her own heart. Vic had been delightful, but he and his surroundings were a passion to be indulged in sparingly, like absinthe, which sooner or later sent the drinker mad.

She supplied Mack with his rabbit, bade him take it outside, and put away all the things she had brought with her. They were now her contribution to the MacAlister Springs establishment. Her own case contained nothing more than some soiled clothes and the little gun. She was glad that she had not had to use it. She laid in the folds of her shirt a handful of the pale alpine flowers, and a piece of bark that had a spicy, strange smell.

Vic came in, slung the stewpot onto the stove, and began to slice onions into it. Phryne possessed herself of some potatoes and a peeling knife, and sat down.

She was getting tired of rabbit stew.

'Well, here we are,' said Dave proudly, 'MacAlister Springs. And a nice little journey, too, no joe blakes.'

'What's a joe blake?' asked Charles faintly. Dave helped him down from his horse and supported him while he got his legs working.

'A snake,' he said. 'I'll just give Vic a cooee.'

'No. I haven't seen him in so long; I want to surprise him. Please. You wait here. I shan't be long.'

Dave said easily, 'All right,' and turned his head. Charles hit him very hard with a rock he had picked up while Dave was supporting him. Dave crumpled to the ground.

Charles walked toward the hut, fumbling for something in his oilskin pocket. The door was open. Mack the dog bounced out, and galloped across to the fallen Dave, whimpering. Charles extracted the thing from his pocket as he reached the door, and stepped over the threshold.

Vic turned from the fire at the step, a greeting on his lips. It died unsaid when he saw the scarecrow standing in the doorway.

Charles had not travelled well. He moved like a mummy, and his face was scratched and his hair torn by branches he had been too clumsy to evade. There was blood on his chin where he had bitten his lip. But what was holding Vic's fascinated attention was the revolver in his hand.

'Charles?' he asked calmly. 'Come in.'

'He is in,' said Phryne, still seated with her lap full of potatoes. 'Charles? Have you gone quite mad?'

'You here?' snarled the man. 'You don't matter. Vic matters.'

'So I see, but why the gun?' asked Phryne in her most irritating drawl. He did not look at her again.

'I've come to kill you,' Charles said on a furious rush of breath. 'You've always been in my way. Even dead, I mean I thought you were dead, she used you to torture me. No! Don't move.' He fired to Vic's right. The shot was dampened by the soft walls. Phryne realized that Charles might easily kill Vic in this mood, once he had completed his gloat. A sudden idea, straight from her guardian angel, struck her. Very slowly, so as not to attract the gunman's attention, she began to bend down so that her hand was near the floor.

'She told me you were fine, a man, not like me. She killed me, Vic, she killed every chance I had at love. I can't love anyone. Not man, not woman.'

'Charlie,' began Vic, holding out a hand.

'No! Don't call me that!' He fired again, and the bullet clanged off a pot and buried itself in the gloom. 'She called me that! She told me, make sure Vic is dead! So I'm making sure! She'll have to love me after this!'

'Wom,' called Phryne softly, hoping that it was dark enough for the creature to build up speed. Charles glanced at her.

'What are you doing?' For a heart-stopping moment the black barrel of the pistol was pointed straight at her head. She left the potato on the floor and sat up.

'Nothing, Charles. Do go on,' she encouraged. He glared. At that moment Wom barrelled across the floor. There were feet in his path; this fact did not impinge on his consciousness of a delicious edible thing on the floor beyond. Wombats are not easily deflected. Wom collected Charles' feet from under him with speed and dispatch, and allowed the body that belonged to them to fall where it would. As it happened, it fell mostly on him.

Phryne jumped on Charles' chest with both knees and directed her peeling knife to his throat.

'Don't even think about moving,' she advised. Charles shut his eyes as the knife grew larger. Vic removed the gun from his loosening grasp at the same time as Dave, recovered from the blow and horrified by shots in this quiet place, burst through the door and tripped over them.

'Ah, Dave,' said Phryne with some difficulty. 'Could you get up, please, I don't really want to drive this knife into Charles' throat, though I am rapidly coming to the view that it might be a good idea. Thank you. Vic, are you all right?'

'Yes. Are you?'

'Yes. Get some rope.'

Dave and Vic secured Charles with a pair of hobbles, binding him hand and foot, and lifting him to reveal Wom still underneath.

'Oh, poor Wom, is he hurt?' cried Phryne. Wom lifted his head to locate the sound, blinked, and continued his destruction of the potato, which this shower of inconvenient humans had rudely interrupted.

Phryne rose from the floor and spread before him the whole netful of potatoes.

Chapter Sixteen

And at night the endless glory of the everlasting stars
Clancy of the Overflow, Banjo Paterson

'This is not quite how I envisaged our last night,' Vic said into Phryne's ear. 'Just you, me, Dave, Mack, and my brother Charlie trussed up in horse hobbles on the floor.'

Phryne turned over in his arms and rested her head on his shoulder.

'You've forgotten Wom under the bed.'

'So I have. And he saved our lives. That was quick thinking, Phryne. Perhaps we'd just better go to sleep.'

'Oh, I think we can manage.' Phryne closed his mouth with a kiss.

Dave slept like a log, rolled in his weatherproof swag with his feet to the fire and a volume of Dickens as a pillow for his bandaged head. Charles lay awake, furious, humiliated, and strained at the ropes that bound his wrists. He heard the faint sounds of flesh sliding against flesh from the big bed, and seethed with outrage.

The worn and greasy rope slipped, and he pulled hard against the knot. His hands were coming free. He waited until he judged that the only unsleeping occupants of the room were engrossed, twisted with an effort that abraded the skin, and managed to free his hands. Swiftly he bent and released his feet.

Then he lay still, thinking furiously. What had Vic done with his gun? He saw it clearly. He had walked ten paces toward the end of the clearing and flung it down. It must still be lying there. All Charles had to do was creep out and he could be in a position of power again. Then they would die; first Vic, then that simpleton Dave, then the dog, then that monstrous grey creature, and last of all Phryne, who had mocked him in his moment of triumph and achieved his downfall by a trick.

Carefully, not whimpering as his stiff muscles cramped and twinged, he got to his knees and began to crawl toward the door. It was not locked. It could not be locked. It opened, like all doors in snow country, inward. Did it creak?

Foot by foot, Charles approached the door and pushed. It did not creak. Then he was over the lintel and out into starlight.

The sky arched, clear and black, and so terribly close that he made an instinctive movement to shield his head. The moon was full and cast an odd blue light, making black pits out of hollows and bleaching the grass silver. Charles was suddenly afraid; the night spoke of death, of limitless space, of the cold beyond the stars that burned with an electric glare just above his head. He cringed, gathered his courage, and began to run for the place where he had seen Vic throw his gun. With a gun he would have divine authority. With a gun he would have the power of a god over life and death.

The door of the hut swung back with a crash. Vic leapt out of bed; Phryne followed, naked and white. Dave woke and jumped up. They all ran to the door and saw Charles heading straight for the chasm that lay at the end of the little meadow, the bottomless abyss where the river was born.

'Charles! Don't! That's the edge of the cliff!' Vic bellowed with the battlefield voice he had never thought he would use again. It had commanded many men to their deaths; it pulled his brother away from the edge as though dragged by a rope. Charles sighted the black depths, heard the river, screamed like an owl and threw himself violently aside. He lost balance, slewed at the brink, and fell backwards, hitting his head on a rock with a small, hollow, soggy, final thump.

Phryne ran with Vic and Dave over the icy grass to the edge. The two men picked up Charles between them. He sagged limply. Phryne had seen that limp sag before. So had Vic.

'It's no use,' he said calmly. 'He's dead. Put him down, Dave.'

Naked, Vic knelt and gathered the body of his dead brother into his arms. Air was expelled from the lungs in one final sigh.

'Poor Charlie,' said Vic. 'You always tried to do what she wanted, and all you could do, in the end, was die in the attempt. No soldier could do more,' he added, laying the body down and closing the staring eyes that bulged, unseeing, up at the moon. Dave stood open-mouthed, averting his gaze from Phryne. She was a silver nymph, he thought, like the lady of Missus Anne's lamp, pure of line and perfectly unmarked. She seemed unaware of her nakedness, so much so that Dave stopped trying not to look at her, since it was evidently a matter of indifference to her whether he looked or not.

'Rest in peace,' said Vic, standing up. 'Get me a tarp from the horse's gear, Dave, we'll wrap him up. Phryne, you must be freezing.'

'No more than you are,' snapped Phryne. 'I'll get some line.'

She fetched a coil of new hemp from the hut, and they trussed and bound the body neatly for carriage.

Phryne threw several lumps of wood on the fire and wrapped herself in her skin rug, and shivered. The death had been so sudden, so unlikely, that she felt bewildered. She had been wondering what to do about Charles; he had solved the problem. And she supposed that it was better to encounter a new hemp rope when you were past worrying about it than to spend a few months contemplating the process of being hanged at the end of it for murdering your brother, his friend, some innocent animals and Miss Phryne Fisher.

She found the brandy bottle and sat down to recover.

Dave and Vic came in. Even in this temperature Vic was not shivering. He found some clothes. Dave took the brandy bottle out of Phryne's clutch.

'Why?' he asked dazedly. 'What was he trying to do? Throw himself off the cliff?'

'No,' said Vic. 'He didn't see the place in proper daylight. Did you tell him that this was just a step in the mountain?'

'No, Vic, why should I? It's obvious.'

'Not to Charles,' said Phryne, reclaiming the bottle. 'He had no interest in scenery and no head for terrain.'

'He saw me throw his gun over the edge, but he didn't know it was the edge,' reasoned Vic. 'He worked himself loose from the hobbles.'

'Who did you get them hobbles from, anyway?' asked Dave. 'Bloody rotten hobbles.'

'Yes. They are. Lucky is always slipping them. He was going for the gun…'

'To account for all of us. A silly thing to do, for without Dave he wouldn't have a snowball's chance in hell of finding his way back to Talbotville, or indeed anywhere. Can I have that bottle, Dave?'

'Yes, he meant to kill us all,' agreed Vic. 'God rest his soul.'

A heavy silence fell.

'Is this going to spoil the place for you?' asked Phryne. Vic took another swallow of brandy and shook his head.

'No. Tomorrow we'll all go back to Talbotville. I'll take the packhorse and Charles. He's my responsibility. We can have the body shipped back to Mother. I wouldn't have liked to give him back to her alive, but dead, she can't do him any more harm. We can report it to the cop at Dargo, explain what happened. With an eminent witness like the Hon. Miss Fisher we shouldn't have any trouble. Then the place will be empty again. Death can't soil this country. It's too big. I'll be all right, Phryne, when you are all gone.'

'Right-ho,' agreed Dave. 'Want me to come along with you?'

'No, you go with Phryne in the plane. She promised you a ride, didn't she?'

'Whacko,' cheered Dave. 'I'll be in that! But how will you go, mate, three days with a corpse?'

'I lived for a year with corpses.' Vic smiled his enchanting smile. 'They don't worry me. And I've got a lot to say to Charlie, and this is my chance of saying it. I'll be fine.'

'Still think you ought to let me make you some hobbles, though,' grumbled Dave, settling down with his feet to the fire again. He appeared to fall instantly asleep.

'Come along,' said Phryne, 'I'm very cold.'

Vic warmed her in his arms and she slept.

Rigel the Gipsy Moth was still tethered to the ground when they reached the Howitt Plains early next morning. Phryne carried her small case, and bunged it into the plane. She hoped that the weather would hold; it was clear and golden and there seemed to be very little wind.

'We have to turn her about,' she explained, hauling on one wing and trundling the Moth in a small circle on her spoked wheels.

'Ain't she light!' marvelled Dave. 'What do I do now?'

'Stand by the prop and be ready to heave it down. Get your hands out of the way smartly then jump in, trying not to make a hole in my wing with those riding boots. On the count of three.'

Phryne started the ignition; to her great relief, the engine fired. She allowed the revs to build up, switched off, counted, and Dave pulled the prop as she switched on again. He vaulted in behind her with lightness and skill, both hands intact.

'Off we go!' screamed Phryne, fervently hoping that this was indeed the case, and Rigel bounced, gained speed, and hopped up into the air over the trees that had scraped her wheels on landing.

Phryne gained height, circling, and sighted MacAlister Springs as a little green patch on the hillside. Vic was waving. She waved back, dipped both wings in salute, and flew off due south, across the Snowy Plains, east over Mount Cynthia, to make her approach down the Crooked River.

She turned her head to see how Dave was faring. Some of her passengers had frozen with fear; most had just frozen. It was very cold but the air was clear. Dave was hanging onto the edges of his seat as updraughts from the valley flicked the Moth across the sky, beaming with delight. He might, Phryne felt, make an airman.

The windsock was limp; no ground wind, so she came in from the fence end of the cleared strip, dropped the Moth neatly into a big puddle which had formed in the interim, and wobbled to a stop.

'Jeez,' said Dave, leaping out and helping Phryne down. 'That was…jeez.'

Phryne was seized by Anne Purvis and Josephine Binet, one on each side, as she waded through the mud. They did not ask questions, but stared very hard.

'Everything is fine,' she assured them. 'I left Vic well.'

They dragged her up onto the road, leaving Dave contemplating the plane in a delighted trance.

'What about his brother?' demanded Anne. 'He went off with Dave four days ago. Where is he?'

'Hell, I expect,' said Phryne shortly. Jo Binet's mouth shut hard on the next question.

'Dave can tell you about it,' she said. 'I have to refuel and get home before I expire from carbon monoxide starvation. He came to kill Vic, and didn't manage it; then he fell and killed himself. Vic is bringing the body down on Dave's packhorse.'

'An accident?' Josephine's eyebrows rose markedly.

Phryne grinned. 'I know, I know. But it really was an accident. If it was murder, do you think Vic would have declined my offer to carry the corpse in the plane, and volunteered to make a three-day journey with a dead man?'

'No,' Josephine decided. 'No. Besides, I can't imagine Vic killing anything. Anne said there was something wrong with the brother. How did he get the chance to try and kill Vic? I'll have the ears off that Dave!'

'He couldn't see Charles as dangerous,' said Phryne. 'He was so very bad at everything Dave knows about. Anyway, we were saved by a wombat. It's a great tale, but I can't stay to tell it. That beautiful blue sky needs a plane in it.'

'How did you leave Vic?' asked Anne. Phryne shrugged.

'He'll be all right, once I have gone and Charles is buried. He says that the mountains aren't soiled by blood.'

'No. But I've never fancied the Wonnangatta homestead.'

'What?'

'You flew over it. You must have seen it. Well, the family that built it died out, one by one, and then the two men living there were murdered. One was found in the river and one on the mountain. No one ever found out who did it.'

'And?'

'Just don't like the feel of the land around there. The air seems heavy.'

'Compared to the air in Poziéres,' said Phryne, 'it would be as clean as an Arctic gale. I must leave, ladies. It has been lovely to meet you. Should you visit the city, my house is yours.'

'Will you be back?' asked Anne.

Phryne blinked. 'I don't know,' she admitted. 'It depends on the hermit. Dave!' she yelled, waking the young man from his trance. 'Your next aviation lesson is called Fuelling the Plane.'

Dave grinned and began hauling the drums from their dump beneath the lee of the riverbank.

Josephine and Anne, with the population of Talbotville, watched the Moth as it circled. They saw the pilot wave, then the plane darted north for the Barry Ranges, and dwindled to a silver speck in an immeasurable blue sky.

'I hope she hasn't done Vic any harm,' worried Anne. Dave turned regretfully from his last glimpse of the plane.

'I reckon she's done him a lot of good,' he said confidently. 'Come into the pub, ladies, and I'll tell you all about it.'

Chapter Seventeen

If you don't like whisky you'd better get used to wine
If'n you don't like whisky you'd better get used to wine
That man he left me with that wine and I feel fine.

'St Louis Blues', W. C. Handy

'Holy willikens!' Bill exclaimed when Phryne landed the Moth back in Melbourne. 'So you did it!'

Yes, she had done it. She had made the return flight with no problems, except for a gusty tailwind which kept trying to blow her off course. She had landed well, and had been smugly gratified by the astounded and blasphemous greeting from Bill.

Mr Butler conveyed her home in her own superb car and handed her over to Dot, who escorted her straight up the stairs. Phryne stripped off the malodorous flying suit, shucked the liquefying boots, and climbed into a very hot bath scented with spruce. She washed her hair, drained and refilled the bath, then lay back, letting the grime and woodsmoke and engine grease soak off her skin, and wondered if she had a decent fingernail to her name.

She stretched out her legs and allowed Dot to scrub her feet. It was very pleasant to be pampered.

'Miss?' asked Dot. Phryne sat up a little before her contentment caused her to drown. Dot was smiling, but looked rather harried.

'Dot dear, tell me about the ball!'

'It was lovely, Miss. I wore the dress and Hugh said I looked beautiful and I danced every dance and ruined me shoes. It was lovely.' Dot smiled reminiscently. 'I danced with the Chief of Police,' she added.

'Really?'

'He stood on my foot.'

'Well, even to have one's foot trodden on by a Chief of Police is a distinction. I got walked on by a wombat.'

'Did you fly all that way, Miss? I was worried! But there was nothing in the newspapers so I knew you were all right.'

'Yes.' Phryne extinguished a chuckle in her face-cloth.

'Did you find the boy, Miss? The one in that photo?'

'Yes, at the top of a mountain. A very nice man, Dot, you'd like him.'

'I think I would,' agreed Dot. 'What happened to that Mr Freeman? He came round here and threw a fit when he heard that you'd gone flying. Mr Butler had to put him out.'

'Well, we won't see him again, Dot.'

Dot scrubbed industriously at Phryne's instep, visibly hesitating before asking her next question.

'Is he...dead, Miss?'

'Yes, and entirely by accident, which is a great relief to us all. No, Dot, don't look at me like that. I promise, it was an accident caused by Charles Freeman all by himself, as God is my witness.'

Dot let go Phryne's foot to cross herself, and sighed.

'God rest his soul,' she said gravely. 'And I don't reckon he's any loss. I liked his brother, though. Is he going to come to the city?'

'No, Dot, I feel sure that he will never come to the city. I may fly up and see him again, sometime. I liked him, too, Dot. But I couldn't stay there, in that cold silence.'

'It would give me the creeps,' agreed Dot, who profoundly distrusted any wilderness more uncharted than the closer city parks. 'There, Miss, that's the best I can do with your feet. There's tar or something on the soles.'

'Sap, I expect. Never mind, it will wear off. Oh, how clean I am and how lovely hot water is! Great invention. No wonder the Romans ruled the world. Give me a hand out of this bath, will you? Otherwise I shall stay here until I dissolve.'

Phryne dried herself on a huge fluffy towel and donned a silk nightgown and a velvet dressing-gown with a collar of rabbit fur. She sat stroking the collar as Dot combed her hair, staring into the mirror at her familiar image, wondering why her eyes did not show the experience of mountains which lay behind them. Her eyes looked back, green and inscrutable as always.

'Any messages, Dot, while I was away?'

'Yes, Miss. Hang on, I've written 'em down. Several gentlemen have been enquiring as to when you would be back, Miss. Mr Lindsay left word that he has finished his exams and asks if you have any towns you want painted red. I haven't the faintest idea what he means, he talks so educated.' Dot was supremely unconscious of irony. 'And Mr Stone, Miss, the musician.'

'Oh?'

'He wanted you to telephone when you came back.'

'Oh, gosh, I'd almost forgotten that problem. Who else?'

'A gentleman who wouldn't leave his name.'

'I know who that is, Dot, a practitioner of the love that dare not speak its name. Tends to demand anonymity.'

This comment went straight over Dot's head, as Phryne had known it would. Dot remembered something and went into the bedroom.

'This came by hand, Miss. There's a label.'

It was a small and rather grubby box, with the superscription, 'Thanks for everything, Percy and Violet.' Inside was a piece of wedding cake.

'That's concluded, then. I hope they'll be very happy. Otherwise this affair is hardly soggy with happy endings, Dot. When we go down for dinner, can you remind me to ask Mrs B for a substantial breakfast? I have to go and tell Mrs Freeman that her bouncing boy and favourite son is dead, and I think I shall need strengthening.'

After completing a beautifully cooked and immaculately served meal in her dining salon, which lacked wombats and hermits, Phryne put herself to bed, and dreamed of flying.

She paused outside Mrs Freeman's door. The document, signed and now dated, in which Victor Ernest Freeman repudiated his inheritance was in her handbag. She had done what she had agreed to do. She took a deep breath, forced her hand into action, and rang the bell.

Mrs Freeman was still on her couch, with attendant and hand-kerchiefs. Phryne whispered to the maid to stay; she did not feel confident of dealing with the vapours on her own. The magnitude of the hysterics which Mrs Freeman would be likely to unleash when she found that her favourite toy was dead was likely to rival a volcanic eruption, the sort that engulfs whole villages in the night.

'Well?'

'I found Victor,' said Phryne. 'He was alive. He is still alive. He has signed this paper, in which he renounces finally and forever any inheritance from his father.' She gave the paper to Mrs Freeman, who read it with voracious eyes.

'Where is Viccy? Why doesn't he come to me?' she wailed. 'Are you sure that this is legal?'

'He will never leave the mountains, Mrs Freeman. And I am assured it is a binding legal document, which he signed of his own free will and in his right mind. He's very happy in the mountains,' she added. Now for the tricky part. Mrs Freeman forestalled her.

'Where is Charles? What have you done with him? He went chasing off to those wretched mountains after you and his brother and I haven't heard from him for a week.'

'Mrs Freeman, I'm afraid that I have bad news,' Phryne began.

The older woman was ahead of her. 'Viccy's alive,' she whispered. 'But Charlie's dead.'

Phryne nodded, thankful to have it out at last. There was a silence.

'He came looking for Vic, intending to kill him. He didn't succeed. Then, in the dark, he fell and hit his head. I saw it and so did a local stockman. Vic is taking the body down to Talbotville on a packhorse. They will have the inquest at Dargo, I expect. It was an accident. Vic didn't kill him.'

'Oh, I know that,' said Mrs Freeman dismissively. 'Vic never could kill things. That's why the war sent him mad. He has a heart of pure marshmallow. You might have killed him, though. Did you?'

'No.'

'So they've all left me now,' she whimpered. 'Charlie and Viccy and Jimmy. I'm a lone, lorn woman.'

'You are also extremely rich and in command of the family company,' Phryne pointed out. Disconcertingly dry eyes fixed her to her chair.

'All my life they wouldn't let me do anything.' Mrs Freeman's voice was still a frail, elderly lady whisper. 'All my life I've been watching them make a mess of things, though Charlie had more talent than his father. He got it from me. You are right, Miss Fisher. I have the family company. And I shall run it. My way.'

A dreadful suspicion struck Phryne and she could not bear to be in the same room as this woman a second longer. She stood up, grasping the arm of the chair. Mrs Freeman saw her face bleach and chuckled.

'You suspect that I sent Charles to kill Vic, hoping that something would happen to him,' she stated.

'Did you?'

'Wouldn't you like to know, young woman,' she cackled. 'Wouldn't you like to know.'

Phryne turned without another word and left the house, ran down the steps to the side of her car, and was luxuriantly and voluptuously sick in the gutter.

Profoundly shocked, she slept the better part of the afternoon, and could face only a boiled egg and toast when she awoke. She called herself roughly to order, reminded herself that people like Mrs Freeman are usually drowned at birth, and dressed for the Jazz Club. Dot handed her stockings and undergarments, and she pulled on a soft Chanel suit and a small, close-fitting hat with a cockade of red feathers. But despite appearances she was not feeling very festive.

Tintagel Stone restored her morale a little. He arrived to collect her looking debonair, well dressed; he could still stir her emotions with his intense blue gaze. She informed him that she had been flying across the alps, and he smiled and made a polite comment but was clearly not interested.

And he was in league with a murderer.

The door to the Jazz Club opened, and the beloved and much missed waft of noise, voices, coffee and cigarettes billowed out and embraced Phryne. Her spirits rose. She plunged inside.

Three musicians were sitting by the kitchen door, arguing about the Meaning of Jazz. It seemed to be the same argument she had heard a week before. Around a table at the front sat the Jazz Makers.

The group on stage finished 'Basin Street Blues', and Nerine stepped down and groped her way to the table.

'Nerine, I have good news for you,' Phryne said, catching at the singer's arm and seating her safely. The skin was satiny beneath her fingers.

Nerine located Phryne and smiled. 'You found that good-for-nothing man of mine?' she asked in her rich accent. Phryne produced the death certificate and Nerine put on her glasses to read it.

'He been gone all this time!' She handed the slip of paper to Ben Rodgers. 'Well, well, well. An' I thought he took a powder.'

'No, he just drank himself to death,' said Phryne. 'Seven years ago. You have been free of him all this time.'

'And I never knew. I thank you, Miss Fisher, that sure is a relief to my mind. Mighty quick work too.' She retrieved the paper from Ben Rodgers and stowed it carefully in her bag, then gave him a long, long look, so loaded with promise that Phryne glanced away. Ben was somewhat short of breath.

'There's something else,' said Iris. 'We have to talk, Miss Fisher.'

'Now?' asked Phryne, gesturing to the rest of the Jazz Makers. Iris nodded.

'All right, if you insist. Now you know that I had been hired to attempt to get Charles Freeman out of trouble,' she said to the band at large, scanning them. Iris, calm and capable. Jim Hyde looking worried. Clarence Davies pausing, coffee cup in hand, with his practised but charming smile. Hugh Anderson tugging doubtfully at his curly hair. Tintagel of the blue eyes intent. Ben Rodgers scowling. Nerine smiling at having been so foolish as to assume that anyone would run away from her lush embrace.

'And the said Charles had a reason for wanting Bernard Stevens, the man who was killed at the Green Mill, dead. Bernard was blackmailing Charles. But Charles didn't do it.'

Silence. Her audience were not giving anything away. Clarence Davies the drummer began to tap the table in a rag-time beat, until Iris flattened his hand with hers. 'Please,' she murmured. Hugh Anderson was staring at Phryne as though she was of an entirely different species.

'It was a difficult problem,' said Phryne, beginning to enjoy herself. 'I never had such a puzzle. The first problem was, how was the man killed? There was no one near enough to stab him but Charles. Charles didn't stab him. Neither did the marathon dancers, nor the lady in puce, nor, of course, I. How, then, was almost as difficult a problem as who and why. There was something different about the body, something had changed, between the time Bernard fell and the time the cops arrived. What? It niggled at the edge of my memory. Then I remembered, finally. The knife had gone, and it was an odd knife. Instead of a proper hilt it had a round handle, like a wooden plug. Unusual for a knife as sharp as this must have been, because it would give no grip – it was only about an inch long. Useless to stab with. But purpose-made to shoot with,' she said, and observed her auditors narrowly. Hugh Anderson blinked. Jim Hyde drew in a breath. The drummer drummed with his fingers again. Iris stared with a puzzled frown. Tintagel Stone looked away. Only Ben Rodgers and Nerine stared straight at Phryne, without moving. Even their stillness was charged with significance.

'So who, I wondered, had removed it? Then I found blood on Tintagel's sleeve. He had withdrawn the knife and hidden it, then smuggled it out of the Green Mill, and I rather think it was in that bottle of wicker-clad Chianti he insists on drinking. Vin trés ordinaire, eh? A very good place to hide a bloody knife. On the spur of the moment, it speaks of a quickness of mind which is rarely to be found. Did Tintagel do it, then? I concluded not. Besides, I don't sleep with murderers if I can avoid it,' added Phryne artlessly. 'Bernard was shot from the front, and he fell, when I came to think of it, with his feet to the band, straight back under the force of the blow, supine, arms outflung. That is how soldiers fall who have been shot through the heart. Who shot him? I considered the front rank of the band. A clarinet is not suitable, and in any case, it is played by Mr Anderson with the bell toward the ground. A trombone is a possibility, but surely the sound would be badly affected if some contrivance was built into the mouth. It would have a muting effect, and Jim Hyde was playing loud and clear. No, it was...'

'Stop!' said Nerine. 'It was me. I killed him.'

They all gazed open-mouthed at her. Under this concentrated regard she shook her head defiantly, and her hair struck coppery sparks in the half-dark. 'He was blackmailing me too.'

'How did you do it?' asked Phryne.

Nerine, clutching at Ben Rodgers as though to keep him in his seat, said rapidly, 'I knew he'd be there. He told me. I changed places with a waitress. I smuggled a gun into the hall through the kitchens. I waited until the lights went down and I stood against the wall, behind the band. No one knew I was there. When everyone was watching the dance marathon, I fired, and I got him.'

'Very nice,' said Phryne. 'But…' She paused. No one spoke. Phryne's lips thinned. Her opinion of trumpeters had been confirmed.

Ben Rodgers had not moved. Only his eyes flicked to one side, as if sizing up a possible retreat.

'No, Nerine, a nice try, but it wasn't you.'

'How do you know?' Nerine's voice was ragged. 'How do you know that thing? Who notices a waitress?'

'Nerine, you couldn't hit the side of a barn with a bucket of bran,' said Jim Hyde patiently. 'I could believe that you wanted to kill the chap, or even that you went there intending to kill him, but not that you took aim in that gloom and hit him in the heart.'

'That does not follow,' said Phryne. 'I saw a little girl in the park do just that, and she had both eyes shut. No, it was Tintagel taking the knife. Why should he do that, if he didn't know you were there? No, good old Ten saw the murder, and he knew who did it and was protecting them. Of course, there is the murder weapon to find and produce. Have you still got it, Tintagel?'

'Yes. I didn't have a chance to get rid of it, what with the cops coming to search, and other distractions,' said Tintagel. 'I've still got it, Miss Fisher.'

'Go on,' said Iris Jordan, intent on the problem. 'Who did it, and how, and why?'

'Do me the favour of going over to those instruments and bringing me the echo cornet,' said Phryne to Hugh, and he obeyed, bringing back the case and opening it.

'This echo cornet,' said Phryne, turning it over, 'has a mute. A special tube; see, here, with its own valve. Might have been designed for the purpose. I don't know what pressure a good trumpeter can build up, but it must be enough to propel a thin knife quite a long way. And land with enough force to kill, if you happen to hit just the right place and don't rebound off a rib. Ben Rodgers, who is so good at metalwork that he makes his own jewellery, didn't find it too hard to modify a stiletto. He could have bought an embroidery stiletto quite legally, though he doesn't quite look the type for needlecraft, and fixed a wooden plug, perhaps a bead, of exactly the right diameter to fit into this narrow opening. It was then just a matter of lifting the cornet, as he invariably does, so that his eyes were almost over the tube, and pressing the valve that cuts in the mute. And striking the wrong man dead at bar thirty-five in "Bye Bye Blackbird".'

'The wrong man?' Hugh Anderson, who had been gnawing his fingernails, uncorked his mouth long enough to speak.

'Yes. He meant to kill…'

'That bastard Charles,' spat Ben Rodgers, leaping to his feet and overturning his chair.

'That bastard, as you say, Charles. Nerine led you to believe that he was chasing her with, er, sexual importunities. Your violent jealousy excites her. As a parlour game it no doubt gave you both a lot of amusement,' said Phryne icily. 'And I would not like to grudge you your fun. Sit down, if you please, Mr Rodgers. I have no patience with tantrums. You see where your indulgence of your temper has led you. I could almost wish that your aim had been better, except that the unlamented Bernard Stevens does not seem to be much of a loss. However, presumably someone loved him, perhaps that poor partner of his who is still in hospital, and even if no one wanted him, you still had no right to kill him. Had you anything against him?'

'No. I didn't even know him,' muttered Rodgers, righting the chair and sitting down again. Nerine had drawn away from him. He put his hand on her shoulder, and she slid under his touch as a cat does under an unwanted caress.

'And Charles? Exactly why did you mark him down for execution?'

'Nerine,' said Ben. 'First I thought that he was giving her the rush, and then it turned out he wanted to steal her from me to sing in another band, and that was worse.'

'And you wanted to smuggle him out of the country so that all blame should fall on him, and not on you? I did not think that disinterested benevolence was one of your virtues.'

'All right. It was me. Now what are you going to do about it? Have you got the cops waiting outside?'

Speaking quietly, Ben was much more threatening. The Jazz Club was buzzing with noise. The group by the door was still wrangling over the nature of jazz, a topic on which every jazz player had an opinion they would defend to the death. Phryne wondered on whom in the band she could rely if Ben attacked her. She wondered most about the delightful Tintagel Stone.

'Do? Me? I shall do nothing about it. I have left a full account of this in safe hands, by the way, so it would not advantage you to lose your temper on me. I was hired merely to free Charles and to find his brother. If a full confession, together with the echo cornet and the murder weapon, is delivered to the police within a reasonable time then I shall have earned my fee. Should you think of melting down the cornet and flinging the knife into the river and denying it all, I am held in sufficient regard by the investigating officer to be able to reconstruct and prove my case anyway.'

Ben Rodgers roared and dived for her. Tintagel, who was nearest, grabbed him by the back of the jacket. Phryne had her little gun ready in her hand. But the stoutest defence came from Nerine, who threw herself in the way and slapped Ben across the face with enough force to make his head snap back.

'Swine!' yelled Nerine at the top of her voice. 'You yellow cur! Ben Rodgers, how dare you! Sit you down this minute and listen to what Miss has to say!'

Ben Rodgers, engorged with wrath, shook his head like a bull struck with an unexpected bandolier. Nerine shoved him back, both hands on his shoulders.

'You and me have things to settle,' she threatened huskily. 'You let me confess. You would have let me be hanged, for that was a good story and could have been true, except Miss Fisher saw through it. You are no gentleman, Ben Rodgers, but that doesn't matter for the moment. You listen! Just you stop bellowing and listen! Did you do it for me, Ben honey?' she asked softly. 'Did you really do it for little me?'

'I did it,' muttered Ben. 'I did it like she said. I made the plug airtight, out of a bead. Like she said. I aimed it and I missed.

I wanted to put out his eye,' he added viciously. 'I practised it, I could hit the ace in the ace of diamonds, but he moved, and the other bloke got in the way.'

Phryne recalled how vaguely her partner Charles had steered her around the floor of the Green Mill, and shivered. It could just as well have been Phryne that Ben Rodgers had shot. She imagined it so vividly that she could almost see the blood stain, the size of a hand, spreading over the back of her pale evening dress. Tintagel Stone had released Ben, now that he seemed subdued. Phryne was refreshed by the fact that he had come to her aid.

'What did you see, Tintagel?' she asked. He winced.

'I heard the "pfft" of the knife from the cornet, saw the flash of silver, saw the chap fall. I knew Ben had done it. When he rushed down to look at the body I slid out the knife and put it in my sleeve, and then, as you say, into the wine bottle. The cops didn't search us that carefully because they knew that we had been playing when it happened. No one else would have thought of him being shot, rather than stabbed. But the shape of the knife was a dead give-away, so I collared it.'

'But why?'

'Why, what?'

'Why protect Ben?'

'He's the best trumpeter in Australia,' said Tintagel, as though his actions were self-explaining, and the Jazz Makers groaned in chorus.

'What did you see, Mr Anderson?'

Hugh removed his thumbnail from between his teeth and said, 'Nothing. I wasn't looking. But I had wondered why Ben looked so stricken, especially when he said he didn't know the chap.'

'All right, then.' Phryne stood up. 'A confession, a rather full and detailed confession, the murder weapon and the cornet delivered to Detective Inspector Robinson in, shall we say, two days? No more than three, anyway. No need to mention your part in it, Tintagel. But get that sleeve cleaned. Do you accept?' she asked formally. Tintagel Stone surveyed Ben, Nerine, and the rest of the group thoughtfully.

'We agree,' he said politely. 'Let me escort you to your car.'

Phryne threaded the maze of tables and found him at her side when she emerged into a cool and bracing night.

'I don't know what to say,' he confessed. Phryne patted his mouth with one forefinger.

'Don't say anything,' she replied. 'Three days at the most, Tintagel.'

'Will I see you again?'

'Do you want to?' came her voice out of the cool darkness. 'I've lost you the best trumpeter in Australia, you know.'

'Even so,' he said, and heard her laugh.

'You may telephone,' she said, and started the big car with a shattering roar that split the never-quiet Fitzroy night.

The Hispano-Suiza slid away. Tintagel Stone turned on his heel and went back into the Jazz Club.

Phryne woke muzzy and haggard, after bad dreams, to the ringing of the phone. Mr Butler answered it, and she heard him come up the stairs and have a brief conversation with Dot at the door of her suite.

Dot came in and pulled back the curtains.

'It's Detective Inspector Robinson on the phone, Miss, and perhaps you'd better talk to him. Mr B says that he sounds wild.'

'Oh, very well,' agreed Phryne, groaning. 'Get me some coffee.'

She swirled down the stairs in a purple dressing-gown and took the receiver from Mr Butler. The hall tiles were chill under her bare feet.

'Miss Fisher?' The voice sounded angry.

'Yes, Jack, it's me.'

'I've just had a delivery.'

'Oh?' Phryne was about to ask whether it had been a happy event and decided not to.

'Yes. This minute. And you had something to do with it.'

'Did I?'

Phryne took the cup of coffee from Dot's hand and sipped.

'Yes.'

'What was this delivery, then?'

'A thing called an echo cornet and a full confession to the murder of Stevens written in a shaky hand on the back of a lot of sheet music for "Bye Bye Blackbird". There was a strange little dart, made to fit into the cornet, as well. Is this your doing?'

'To a certain extent. I was hired, you know, to get Charles Freeman out of the jug, and I did tell you that I would reveal all. I was going to do that today.'

'So you knew that it was Ben Rodgers.'

'Yes.'

'You've allowed a murderer to escape, you know that?' the policeman roared. 'You must have told 'em last night, them Jazz Makers.'

'Well?' Phryne was getting cold and had finished her coffee. 'What happened to Rodgers?'

'He's vanished. He could have shipped aboard any of half a dozen tramps going all over the world. I ought to run you in for obstructing the course of justice, so I ought.'

'Try,' said Phryne icily. Silence fell on the other end of the line. Phryne could imagine the boiling fury Jack Robinson must be feeling, and wondered what he was going to do. She felt slighted. She had found his murderer for him, and arranged for a confession and the evidence to be delivered to his very door. She had spared him the humiliation of an unsolved case and had pointed him unequivocally toward the right man. Was she to be blamed for not capturing Ben Rodgers and binding him hand and foot? Were the police to have it all their own way? Besides, she had partly done it for Nerine. Phryne liked Nerine, although she made Phryne feel so plain.

Ben Rodgers would have taken Nerine with him. And Charles Freeman was dead by what was near enough to his own hand, and all in all it seemed to Phryne as close to a happy ending as could be expected in an imperfect world.

'Well, er,' said Jack Robinson, jolting Phryne out of her reverie, 'er, well, yes. We should have been watching him, I suppose. We've put out an all-ports warning, so we should get him all right.'

That was as close as Phryne was going to get to thanks or apology, so she murmured a goodbye and hung up. She decided to go back to bed and see if more sleep would improve her mood.

As she was leaving the hall the phone rang and it was Jack Robinson again.

'By the bye,' he sounded more controlled, 'that band leader is in the clear. The confession says that it was all Rodgers' own idea. And it appears that it was not Bernard Stevens, but your Charles Freeman that he was trying to kill. What happened to him, is he back with his mum?'

'No, he's dead. He died in an accident, in the mountains. He was looking for his brother.'

'His brother? Did he find him?'

'No,' said Phryne with finality. 'No one will ever find him now.'

And she trailed up the stairs and put herself back to bed.

That evening she dressed for the Jazz Club again. More music was needed to take the taste of murder and lost mountain men out of her mouth.

Tintagel was pleasant, with a sense of release which Phryne accounted for by the escape of Ben Rodgers.

That he had escaped was fairly plain. He had made the arrangements for Charles; he had merely to take advantage of them himself. Phryne wondered if Tintagel was angry with her.

'Tintagel, are you furious with me for losing you the best trumpeter in Australia?'

'No, Phryne, I'm not. Couldn't be helped.'

'Why are you so pleased with yourself?' she asked, and watched his mouth curve into a secret smile.

'You'll see,' he promised.

The usual group was sitting at the usual table; it included a back which was familiar. Nerine turned her blind eyes toward

Phryne as she was seated beside her by the hovering Tintagel Stone.

Nerine had been weeping for hours. Ben Rodgers had gone and abandoned her. Phryne was mortified. The bastard, she thought, the cold-blooded bastard. He's left her and run like a rabbit, and I could have handed him over to the law. I should have let him hang.

'Oh, Nerine, I'm so sorry…' she began, and the singer smiled a wobbly smile.

'It ain't none of your doin', honey,' she said in her beautiful voice. 'That rat of a man has taken a run-out powder and I reckon by now he's in New Orleans. Don't you pay it no never-mind, honey.'

'Miss Fisher, this is Tim Stamp, our new cornet player.'

He was young and fresh-faced, with short, curly red hair, and he blushed whenever one of the group addressed him.

'You've got a new trumpeter already?'

'Yes. Pity about Ben but he really was a beast to play with. Hogged the centre, upstaged poor Jim, had a savage tongue.'

'And he killed people,' Phryne reminded him.

'Yes, that too,' agreed Tintagel absently. 'Tim, this is Miss Fisher, who is indirectly responsible for us being short a trumpeter. Would you like to show her how you can play?'

Tim Stamp took Phryne's hand and then did not seem to know what to do with it. Phryne decided to take it back. The young man unearthed his trumpet from under a pile of gear and touched Nerine respectfully on the shoulder. She put her hand on his arm and was led onto the stage.

The room fell silent. Tim Stamp raised the trumpet and began 'Downhearted Blues'. He was not as brash and authoritative as Ben Rodgers had been, but the tone was sweeter, softer, and he placed each note exactly. Nerine blinked her reddened eyes and lifted both hands to her breast.

'I've got the downhearted blues,' she sang, with such power that Phryne was forced back in her seat. Tim's trumpet embroidered behind the voice, never demanding, never intruding. Tintagel gripped Phryne's hand.

'Isn't she amazing?' he breathed. Concentrated sorrow flowed from the stage. Conversation stopped. Impossible to order coffee or complain about the service when Nerine was tearing her heart to pieces and strewing it like confetti.

'I ain't never loved but three men in my life,' she sang to the entranced audience, who did not dare move. ''Twas my father and my brother.' She paused while the trumpet wove a melody around the next note. The concluding line came with biblical force: 'And the man who wrecked my life.'

'How long can she go on like this?' Phryne whispered. 'She'll do herself an injury!'

'No, no, listen.' Tintagel was enthralled. Nerine reached the last verse.

'I walked that floor, and I wrung my hands and cried,' she mourned. 'Got the downhearted blues and cain't be,' a breath, a wail from the trumpet, 'satisfied,' she concluded. The room rocked with applause.

'I may have lost the best cornet player in Australia,' said Tintagel proudly, 'but I've got the best blues singer in the world.'

'She's remarkable,' agreed Phryne as Nerine began on 'Empty Bed Blues'. Tintagel listened, entranced. Phryne put her hand on his sleeve, still obscurely troubled about his degree of complicity.

'Pity about Ben,' she suggested softly, as Nerine and the trumpet came down an excruciating tone, reeking of despair.

He replied absently, 'Yes, I should never have let him try it at the Green Mill,' and then snapped out of the song. Blue eyes like a blowtorch met Phryne's green gaze.

'You knew he was going to do it,' she said.

'Yes,' he answered simply. His hand closed over hers, tight enough to hurt.

'I thought so.'

'What are you going to do?' he asked.

Phryne considered. 'Listen to the music,' she replied.

Nerine concluded the song, and wavered down to the floor again. She picked up Tintagel's coffee and drained it at a gulp.

'I reckon I owe that bastard Ben this, anyway,' she reflected without a smile.

'What?' said Phryne, her hand still clasped in Tintagel's. She was shaken by his confession, and profoundly disturbed by Nerine's despair.

'He taught me how to sing the blues,' said Nerine. 'Tim, honey, get me some coffee. Yes,' she added, patting the clasped hands, 'he taught me to sing the blues real good.'

Phryne let go the breath she had been holding and started to laugh.

To receive a free catalog of Poisoned Pen Press titles, please provide your name, address, and e-mail address in one of the following ways:

Phone: 1-800-421-3976
Facsimile: 1-480-949-1707
Email: info@poisonedpenpress.com
Website: www.poisonedpenpress.com

Poisoned Pen Press
6962 E. First Ave. Ste 103
Scottsdale, AZ 85251